THE PIGEON PIE

Charlotte M. Yonge

1st WORLD
LIBRARY
Literary Society

Pigeon Pie

Charlotte M. Yonge

© 1st World Library – Literary Society, 2005
PO Box 2211
Fairfield, IA 52556
www.1stworldlibrary.org
First Edition

LCCN: 2004195596

Softcover ISBN: 1-4218-0417-4
Hardcover ISBN: 1-4218-0317-8
eBook ISBN: 1-4218-0517-0

Purchase *"Pigeon Pie"*
as a traditional bound book at:
www.1stWorldLibrary.org/purchase.asp?ISBN=1-4218-0417-4

Pigeon Pie
contributed by Tim, Ed & Rodney
in support of
1st World Library Literary Society

CHAPTER I.

Early in the September of the year 1651 the afternoon sun was shining pleasantly into the dining-hall of Forest Lea House. The sunshine came through a large bay-window, glazed in diamonds, and with long branches of a vine trailing across it, but in parts the glass had been broken and had never been mended. The walls were wainscoted with dark oak, as well as the floor, which shone bright with rubbing, and stag's antlers projected from them, on which hung a sword in its sheath, one or two odd gauntlets, an old-fashioned helmet, a gun, some bows and arrows, and two of the broad shady hats then in use, one with a drooping black feather, the other plainer and a good deal the worse for wear, both of a small size, as if belonging to a young boy.

An oaken screen crossed the hall, close to the front door, and there was a large open fireplace, a settle on each side under the great yawning chimney, where however at present no fire was burning. Before it was a long dining-table covered towards the upper end with a delicately white cloth, on which stood, however, a few trenchers, plain drinking-horns, and a large old-fashioned black-jack, that is to say, a pitcher formed of leather. An armchair was at the head of the table, and heavy oaken benches along the side.

A little boy of six years old sat astride on the end of one of the benches, round which he had thrown a bridle of plaited rushes, and, with a switch in his other hand, was springing himself up and down, calling out, "Come, Eleanor, come, Lucy; come and ride on a pillion behind me to Worcester, to see King Charles and brother Edmund."

"I'll come, I am coming!" cried Eleanor, a little girl about a year older, her hair put tightly away under a plain round cap, and she was soon perched sideways behind her brother.

"Oh, fie, Mistress Eleanor; why, you would not ride to the wars?" This was said by a woman of about four or five-and-twenty, tall, thin and spare, with a high colour, sharp black eyes, and a waist which the long stiff stays, laced in front, had pinched in till it was not much bigger than a wasp's, while her quilted green petticoat, standing out full below it, showed a very trim pair of ankles encased in scarlet stockings, and a pair of bony red arms came forth from the full short sleeves of a sort of white jacket, gathered in at the waist. She was clattering backwards and forwards, removing the dinner things, and talking to the children as she did so in a sharp shrill tone: "Such a racket as you make, to be sure, and how you can have the heart to do so I can't guess, not I, considering what may be doing this very moment."

"Oh, but Walter says they will all come back again, brother Edmund, and Diggory, and all," said little Eleanor, "and then we shall be merry."

"Yes," said Lucy, who, though two years older, wore the same prim round cap and long frock as her little

Charlotte M. Yonge

sister, "then we shall have Edmund here again. You can't remember him at all, Eleanor and Charlie, for we have not seen him these six years!"

"No," said Deborah, the maid. "Ah! these be weary wars, what won't let a gentleman live at home in peace, nor his poor servants, who have no call to them."

"For shame, Deb!" cried Lucy; "are not you the King's own subject?"

But Deborah maundered on, "It is all very well for gentlefolks, but now it had all got quiet again, 'tis mortal hard it should be stirred up afresh, and a poor soul marched off, he don't know where, to fight with he don't know who, for he don't know what."

"He ought to know what!" exclaimed Lucy, growing very angry. "I tell you, Deb, I only wish I was a man! I would take the great two-handled sword, and fight in the very front rank for our Church and our King! You would soon see what a brave cavalier's daughter - son I mean," said Lucy, getting into a puzzle, "could do."

The more eager Lucy grew, the more unhappy Deborah was, and putting her apron to her eyes, she said in a dismal voice, "Ah! 'tis little poor Diggory wots of kings and cavaliers!"

What Lucy's indignation would have led her to say next can never be known, for at this moment in bounced a tall slim boy of thirteen, his long curling locks streaming tangled behind him. "Hollo!" he shouted, "what is the matter now? Dainty Deborah in the dumps? Cheer up, my lass! I'll warrant that doughty Diggory is discreet enough to encounter no more bullets than he can reasonably avoid!"

This made Deborah throw down her apron and reply, with a toss of the head, "None of your nonsense, Master Walter, unless you would have me speak to my lady. Cry for Diggory, indeed!"

"She was really crying for him, Walter," interposed Lucy.

"Mistress Lucy!" exclaimed Deborah, angrily, "the life I lead among you is enough -"

"Not enough to teach you good temper," said Walter. "Do you want a little more?"

"I wish someone was here to teach you good manners," answered the tormented Deborah. "As if it was not enough for one poor girl to have the work of ten servants on her hands, here must you be mock, mock, jeer, jeer, worrit, worrit, all day long! I had rather be a mark for all the musketeers in the Parliamentary army."

This Deborah always said when she was out of temper, and it therefore made Walter and Lucy laugh the more; but in the midst of their merriment in came a girl of sixteen or seventeen, tall and graceful. Her head was bare, her hair fastened in a knot behind, and in little curls round her face; she had an open bodice of green silk, and a white dress under it, very plain and neat; her step was quick and active, but her large dark eyes had a grave thoughtful look, as if she was one who would naturally have loved to sit still and think, better than to bustle about and be busy. Eleanor ran up to her at once, complaining that Walter was teasing Deborah shamefully. She was going to speak, but Deborah cut her short.

"No Mistress Rose, I will not have even you excuse him, I'll go and tell my lady how a poor faithful wench is served;" and away she flounced, followed by Rose.

"Will she tell mamma?" asked little Charlie.

"Oh no, Rose will pacify her," said Lucy.

"I am sure I wish she would tell," said Eleanor, a much graver little person than Lucy; "Walter is too bad."

"It is only to save Diggory the trouble of taking a crabstick to her when he returns from the wars," said Walter. "Heigh ho!" and he threw himself on the bench, and drummed on the table. "I wish I was there! I wonder what is doing at Worcester this minute!"

"When will brother Edmund come?" asked Charlie for about the hundredth time.

"When the battle is fought, and the battle is won, and King Charles enjoys his own again! Hurrah!" shouted Walter, jumping up, and beginning to sing -

>   "For forty years our royal throne
>   Has been his father's and his own."

Lucy joined in with -

>   "Nor is there anyone but he
>   With right can there a sharer be."

"How can you make such a noise?" said Eleanor,

stopping her ears, by which she provoked Walter to go on roaring into them, while he pulled down her hand -

"For who better may
The right sceptre sway
Than he whose right it is to reign;
Then look for no peace,
For the war will never cease
Till the King enjoys his own again."

As he came to the last line, Rose returning exclaimed, "Oh, hush, Lucy. Pray don't, Walter!"

"Ha! Rose turned Roundhead?" cried Walter. "You don't deserve to hear the good news from Worcester."

"O, what?" cried the girls, eagerly.

"When it comes," said Walter, delighted to have taken in Rose herself; but Rose, going up to him gently, implored him to be quiet, and listen to her.

"All this noisy rejoicing grieves our mother," said she. "If you could but have seen her yesterday evening, when she heard your loyal songs. She sighed, and said, 'Poor fellow, how high his hopes are!' and then she talked of our father and that evening before the fight at Naseby."

Walter looked grave and said, "I remember! My father lifted me on the table to drink King Charles's health, and Prince Rupert - I remember his scarlet mantle and white plume - patted my head, and called me his little cavalier."

"We sat apart with mother," said Rose, "and heard the

loud cheers and songs till we were half frightened at the noise."

"I can't recollect all that," said Lucy.

"At least you ought not to forget how our dear father came in with Edmund, and kissed us, and bade mother keep up a good heart. Don't you remember that, Lucy?"

"I do," said Walter; "it was the last time we ever saw him."

And Walter sat on the table, resting one foot on the bench, while the other dangled down, and leaning his elbow on his knee and his head on his hand; Rose sat on the bench close by him, with Charlie on her lap, and the two little girls pressing close against her, all earnest to hear from her the story of the great fight of Naseby, where they had all been in a farmhouse about a mile from the field of battle.

"I don't forget how the cannon roared all day," said Lucy.

"Ah! that dismal day!" said Rose. "Then by came our troopers, blood-stained and disorderly, riding so fast that scarcely one waited to tell my mother that the day was lost and she had better fly. But not a step did she stir from the gate, where she stood with you, Charlie, in her arms; she only asked of each as he passed if he had seen my father or Edmund, and ever her cheek grew whiter and whiter. At last came a Parliament officer on horseback - it was Mr. Enderby, who had been a college mate of my father's, and he told us that my dear father was wounded, and had sent him to fetch her."

"But I never knew where Edmund was then," said Eleanor. "No one ever told me."

"Edmund lifted up my father when he fell," said Walter, "and was trying to bind his wound; but when Colonel Enderby's troop was close upon them, my father charged him upon his duty to fly, saying that he should fall into the hands of an old friend, and it was Edmund's duty to save himself to fight for the King another time."

"So Edmund followed Prince Rupert?" said Eleanor.

"Yes," said Lucy; "you know my father once saved Prince Rupert's life in the skirmish where his horse was killed, so for his sake the Prince made Edmund his page, and has had him with him in all his voyages and wanderings. But go on about our father, Rose. Did we go to see him?"

"No; Mr. Enderby said he was too far off, so he left a trooper to guard us, and my mother only took her little babe with her. Don't you remember, Walter, how Eleanor screamed after her, as she rode away on the colonel's horse; and how we could not comfort the little ones, till they had cried themselves to sleep, poor little things? And in the morning she came back, and told us our dear father was dead! O Walter, how can we look back to that day, and rejoice in a new war? How can you wonder her heart should sink at sounds of joy which have so often ended in tears?"

Walter twisted about and muttered, but he could not resist his sister's earnest face and tearful eyes, and said something about not making so much noise in the house.

"There's my own dear brother," said Rose. "And you won't tease Deborah?"

"That is too much, Rose. It is all the sport I have, to see the faces she makes when I plague her about Diggory. Besides, it serves her right for having such a temper."

"She has not a good temper, poor thing!" said Rose; "but if you would only think how true and honest she is, how hard she toils, and how ill she fares, and yet how steadily she holds to us, you would surely not plague and torment her."

Rose was interrupted by a great outcry, and in rushed Deborah, screaming out, "Lack-a-day! Mistress Rose! O Master Walter! what will become of us? The fight is lost, the King fled, and a whole regiment of red-coats burning and plundering the whole country. Our throats will be cut, every one of them!"

"You'll have a chance of being a mark for all the musketeers in the Parliament army," said Walter, who even then could not miss a piece of mischief.

"Joking now, Master Walter!" cried Deborah, very much shocked. "That is what I call downright sinful. I hope you'll be made a mark of yourself, that I do."

The children were running off to tell their mother, when Rose stopped them, and desired to know how Deborah had heard the tidings. It was from two little children from the village who had come to bring a present of some pigeons to my lady. Rose went herself to examine the children, but she could only learn that a packman had come into the village and brought the report that the King had been defeated, and had fled from the field. They knew no more, and Walter pronouncing it to be all a cock-and-bull story of some rascally prick-eared pedlar, declared he would go down to the village and enquire into the rights of it.

These were the saddest times of English history, when the wrong cause had been permitted for a time to triumph, and the true and rightful side was persecuted; and among those who endured affliction for the sake of their Church and their King, none suffered more, or more patiently, than Lady Woodley, or, as she was called in the old English fashion, Dame Mary Woodley, of Forest Lea.

When first the war broke out she was living happily in her pleasant home with her husband and children; but when King Charles raised his standard at Nottingham, all this comfort and happiness had to be given up. Sir Walter Woodley joined the royal army, and it soon became unsafe for his wife and children to remain at home, so that they were forced to go about with him, and suffer all the hardships of the sieges and battles. Lady Woodley was never strong, and her health was very much hurt by all she went through; she was almost always unwell, and if Rose, though then quite a child, had not shown care and sense beyond her years for the little ones, it would be hard to say what would have become of them.

Yet all she endured while dragging about her little babies through the country, with bad or insufficient food, uncomfortable lodgings, pain, weariness and anxiety, would have been as nothing but for the heavy

Charlotte M. Yonge

sorrows that came upon her also. First she lost her only brother, Edmund Mowbray, and in the battle of Naseby her husband was killed; besides which there were the sorrows of the whole nation in seeing the King sold, insulted, misused, and finally slain, by his own subjects. After Sir Walter's death, Lady Woodley went home with her five younger children to her father's house at Forest Lea; for her husband's estate, Edmund's own inheritance, had been seized and sequestrated by the rebels. She was the heiress of Forest Lea since the loss of her brother, but the old Mr. Mowbray, her father, had given almost all his wealth for the royal cause, and had been oppressed by the exactions of the rebels, so that he had nothing to leave his daughter but the desolate old house and a few bare acres of land. For the shelter, however, Lady Woodley was very thankful; and there she lived with her children and a faithful servant, Deborah, whose family had always served the Mowbrays, and who would not desert their daughter now.

The neighbours in the village loved, and were sorry for, their lady, and used to send her little presents; there was a large garden in which Diggory Stokes, who had also served her father, raised vegetables for her use; the cow wandered in the deserted park, and so they contrived to find food; while all the work of the house was done by Rose and Deborah. Rose was her mother's great comfort, nursing her, cheering her, taking care of the little ones, teaching them, working for them, and making light of all her exertions. Everyone in the village loved Rose Woodley, for everyone had in some way been helped or cheered by her. Her mother was only sometimes afraid she worked too hard, and would try her strength too much; but she was always bright and cheerful, and when the day's work was done no one was more gay and lively and ready for play with the little ones.

Rose had more trial than anyone knew with Deborah. Deborah was as faithful as possible, and bore a great deal for the sake of her mistress, worked hard day and night, had little to eat and no wages, yet lived on with them rather than forsake her dear lady and the children. One thing, however, Deborah would not do, and that was to learn to rule her tongue and her temper. She did not know, nor do many excellent servants, how much trial and discomfort she gave to those she loved so earnestly, by her constant bursting out into hasty words whenever she was vexed - her grumbling about whatever she disliked, and her ill-judged scolding of the children. Servants in those days were allowed to speak more freely to their masters and mistresses than at present, so that Deborah had more opportunity of making such speeches, and it was Rose's continual work to try to keep her temper from being fretted, or Lady Woodley from being teased with her complaints. Rose was very forbearing, and but for this there would have been little peace in the house.

Walter was thirteen, an age when it is not easy to keep boys in order, unless they will do so for themselves. Though a brave generous boy, he was often unruly and inconsiderate, apt not to obey, and to do what he knew to be unkind or wrong, just for the sake of present amusement. He was thus his mother's great anxiety, for she knew that she was not fit either to teach or to restrain him, and she feared that his present wild disobedient ways might hurt his character for ever, and lead to dispositions which would in time swallow up all the good about him, and make him what he would now tremble to think of.

She used to talk of her anxieties to Doctor Bathurst, the good old clergyman who had been driven away from his parish, but used to come in secret to help, teach, and use his ministry for the faithful ones of his flock. He would tell her that while she did her best for her son, she must trust the rest to his FATHER above, and she might do so hopefully, since it had been in His own cause that the boy had been made fatherless. Then he would speak to Walter, showing him how wrong and how cruel were his overbearing, disobedient ways. Walter was grieved, and resolved to improve and become steadier, that he might be a comfort and blessing to his mother; but in his love of fun and mischief he was apt to forget himself, and then drove away what might have been in time repentance and improvement, by fancying he did no harm. Teasing Deborah served her right, he would tell himself, she was so ill-tempered and foolish; Diggory was a clod, and would do nothing without scolding; it was a good joke to tease Charlie; Eleanor was a vexatious little thing, and he would not be ordered by her; so he went his own way, and taught the merry chattering Lucy to be very nearly as bad as himself, neglected his duties, set a bad example, tormented a faithful servant, and seriously distressed his mother. Give him some great cause, he thought, and he would be the first and the best, bring back the King, protect his mother and sisters, and perform glorious deeds, such as would make his name be remembered for ever. Then it would be seen what he was worth; in the meantime he lived a dull life, with nothing to do, and he must have some fun. It did not signify if he was not particular about little things, they were women's affairs, and all very well for Rose, but when some really important matter came, that would be his time for distinguishing himself.

In the meantime Charles II. had been invited to Scotland, and had brought with him, as an attendant, Edmund Woodley, the eldest son. As soon as he was known to have entered England, some of the loyal gentlemen of the neighbourhood of Forest Lea went to join the King, and among their followers went Farmer Ewins, who had fought bravely in the former war under Edmund Mowbray, several other of the men of the village, and lastly, Diggory Stokes, Lady Woodley's serving man, who had lately shown symptoms of discontent with his place, and fancied that as a soldier he might fare better, make his fortune, and come home prosperously to marry his sweetheart, Deborah.

CHAPTER II.

Walter ran down to the village at full speed. He first bent his steps towards the "Half-Moon," the little public-house, where news was sure to be met with. As he came towards it, however, he heard the loud sound of a man's voice going steadily on as if with some discourse. "Some preachment," said he to himself: "they've got a thorough-going Roundhead, I can hear his twang through his nose! Shall I go in or not?"

While he was asking himself this question, an old peasant in a round frock came towards him.

"Hollo, Will!" shouted Walter, "what prick-eared rogue have you got there?"

"Hush, hush, Master Walter!" said the old man, taking off his hat very respectfully. "Best take care what you say, there be plenty of red-coats about. There's one of them now preaching away in marvellous pied words. It is downright shocking to hear the Bible hollaed out after that sort, so I came away. Don't you go nigh him, sir, 'specially with your hat set on in that -"

"Never mind my hat," said Walter, impatiently, "it is no business of yours, and I'll wear it as I please in spite of old Noll and all his crew."

For his forefathers' sake, and for the love of his mother and sister, the good village people bore with Walter's haughtiness and discourtesy far more than was good for him, and the old man did not show how much he was hurt by his rough reception of his good advice. Walter was not reminded that he ought to rise up before the hoary head, and reverence the old man, and went on hastily, "But tell me, Will, what do you hear of the battle?"

"The battle, sir! why, they say it is lost. That's what the fellow there is preaching about."

"And where was it? Did you hear? Don't you know?"

"Don't be so hasty, don't ye, sir!" said the old slow-spoken man, growing confused. "Where was it? At some town - some town, they said, but I don't know rightly the name of it."

"And the King? Who was it? Not Cromwell? Had Lord Derby joined?" cried Walter, hurrying on his questions so as to puzzle and confuse the old man more and more, till at last he grew angry at getting no explanation, and vowed it was no use to talk to such an old fool. At that moment a sound as of feet and horses came along the road. "'Tis the soldiers!" said Walter.

"Ay, sir, best get out of sight."

Walter thought so too, and, springing over a hedge, ran off into a neighbouring wood, resolving to take a turn, and come back by the longer way to the house, so as to avoid the road. He walked across the wood, looking up at the ripening nuts, and now and then springing up to reach one, telling himself all the time that it was untrue, and that the King could not, and should not be defeated. The wood grew less thick after a time, and ended in low brushwood, upon an open common. Just as Walter was coming to this place, he saw an unusual sight: a man and a horse crossing the down. Slowly and wearily they came, the horse drooping its head and stumbling in its pace, as though worn out with fatigue, but he saw that it was a war-horse, and the saddle and other equipments were such as he well remembered in the royal army long ago. The rider wore buff coat, cuirass, gauntlets guarded with steel, sword, and pistols, and Walter's first impulse was to avoid him; but on giving a second glance, he changed his mind, for though there was neither scarf, plume, nor any badge of party, the long locks, the set of the hat, and the general air of the soldier were not those of a rebel. He must be a cavalier, but, alas! far unlike the triumphant cavaliers whom Walter had hoped to receive, for he was covered with dust and blood, as if he had fought and ridden hard. Walter sprung forward to meet him, and saw that he was a young man, with dark eyes and hair, looking very pale and exhausted, and both he and his horse seemed hardly able to stir a step further.

"Young sir," said the stranger, "what place is this? Am I near Forest Lea?"

A flash of joy crossed Walter. "Edmund! are you Edmund?" he exclaimed, colouring deeply, and looking up in his face with one quick glance, then casting down his eyes.

"And you are little Walter," returned the cavalier, instantly dismounting, and flinging his arm around his brother; "why, what a fine fellow you are grown! How are my mother and all?"

"Well, quite well!" cried Walter, in a transport of joy. "Oh! how happy she will be! Come, make haste home!"

"Alas! I dare not as yet. I must not enter the house till nightfall, or I should bring danger on you all. Are there any troopers near?"

"Yes, the village is full of the rascals. But what has happened? It is not true that -" He could not bear to say the rest.

"Too true!" said Edmund, leading his tired horse within the shelter of the bushes. "It is all over with us!"

"The battle lost!" said Walter, in a stifled tone; and in all the bitterness of the first disappointment of his youth, he turned away, overcome by a gush of tears and sobs, stamping as he walked up and down, partly with the intensity of his grief, partly with shame at being seen by his brother, in tears.

"Had you set your heart on it so much?" said Edmund, kindly, pleased to see his young brother so ardent a loyalist. "Poor fellow! But at least the King was safe when I parted from him. Come, cheer up, Walter, the right will be uppermost some day or other."

"But, oh, that battle! I had so longed to see old Noll get his deserts," said Walter, "I made so sure. But how did it happen, Edmund?"

"I cannot tell you all now, Walter. You must find me some covert where I can be till night fall. The rebels

Charlotte M. Yonge

are hot in pursuit of all the fugitives. I have ridden from Worcester by byroads day and night, and I am fairly spent. I must be off to France or Holland as soon as may be, for my life is not safe a moment here. Cromwell is bitterer than ever against all honest men, but I could not help coming this way, I so much longed to see my mother and all of you."

"You are not wounded?" said Walter, anxiously.

"Nothing to speak of, only a sword-cut on my shoulder, by which I have lost more blood than convenient for such a journey."

"Here, I'll lead your horse; lean on me," said Walter, alarmed at the faint, weary voice in which his brother spoke after the first excitement of the recognition. "I'll show you what Lucy and I call our bower, where no one ever comes but ourselves. There you can rest till night."

"And poor Bayard?" said Edmund.

"I think I could put him into the out-house in the field next to the copse, hide his trappings here, and get him provender from Ewins's farm. Will that do?"

"Excellently. Poor Ewins! - that is a sad story. He fell, fighting bravely by my side, cut down in Sidbury Street in the last charge. Alas! these are evil days!"

"And Diggory Stokes, our own knave?"

"I know nothing of him after the first onset. Rogues and cowards enough were there. Think, Walter, of seeing his Majesty strive in vain to rally them, when the day might yet have been saved, and the traitors hung down their heads, and stood like blocks while he called on them rather to shoot him dead than let him live to see such a day!"

"Oh, had I but been there, to turn them all to shame!"

"There were a few, Walter; Lord Cleveland, Hamilton, Careless, Giffard, and a few more of us, charged down Sidbury Street, and broke into the ranks of the rebels, while the King had time to make off by S. Martin's Gate. Oh, how I longed for a few more! But the King was saved so far; Careless, Giffard, and I came up with him again, and we parted at nightfall. Lord Derby's counsel was that he should seek shelter at Boscobel, and he was to disguise himself, and go thither under Giffard's guidance. Heaven guard him, whatever becomes of us!"

"Amen!" said Walter, earnestly. "And here we are. Here is Lucy's bank of turf, and my throne, and here we will wait till the sun is down."

It was a beautiful green slope, covered with soft grass, short thyme, and cushion-like moss, and overshadowed by a thick, dark yew-tree, shut in by brushwood on all sides, and forming just such a retreat as children love to call their own. Edmund threw himself down at full length on it, laid aside his hat, and passed his hand across his weary forehead. "How quiet!" said he; "but, hark! is that the bubbling of water?" he added, raising himself eagerly.

"Yes, here," said Walter, showing him where, a little further off on the same slope, a little clear spring rose in a natural basin of red earth, fringed along the top

Charlotte M. Yonge

with fresh green mosses.

"Delicious!" said the tired soldier, kneeling over the spring, scooping it up in his hand to drink, opening his collar, and bathing hands and face in the clear cool fountain, till his long black hair hung straight, saturated with wet.

"Now, Bayard, it is your turn," and he patted the good steed as it sucked up the refreshing water, and Walter proceeded to release it from saddle and bridle. Edmund, meanwhile, stretched himself out on the mossy bank, asked a few questions about his mother, Rose, and the other children, but was too tired to say much, and presently fell sound asleep, while Walter sat by watching him, grieving for the battle lost, but proud and important in being the guardian of his brother's safety, and delighting himself with the thought of bringing him home at night.

More was happening at home than Walter guessed. The time of his absence seemed very long, more especially when the twilight began to close in, and Lady Woodley began to fear that he might, with his rashness, have involved himself in some quarrel with the troopers in the village. Lady Woodley and her children had closed around the wood fire which had been lighted on the hearth at the approach of evening, and Rose was trying by the bad light to continue her darning of stockings, when a loud hasty knocking was heard at the door, and all, in a general vague impression of dread, started and drew together.

"Oh my lady!" cried Deborah, "don't bid me go to the door, I could not if you offered me fifty gold caroluses! I had rather stand up to be a mark -"

"Then I will," said Rose, advancing.

"No, no, Mistress Rose," said Deborah, running forward. "Don't I know what is fit for the like of you? You go opening the door to rogues and vagabonds, indeed!" and with these words she undrew the bolts and opened the door.

"Is this the way you keep us waiting?" said an impatient voice; and a tall youth, handsomely accoutred, advanced authoritatively into the room. "Prepare to -" but as he saw himself alone with women and children, and his eyes fell on the pale face, mourning dress, and graceful air of the lady of the house, he changed his tone, removed his hat, and said, "Your pardon, madam, I came to ask a night's lodging for my father, who has been thrown from his horse, and badly bruised."

"I cannot refuse you, sir," said Lady Woodley, who instantly perceived that this was an officer of the Parliamentary force, and was only thankful to see that he was a gentleman, and enforced with courtesy a request which was in effect a command.

The youth turned and went out, while Lady Woodley hastily directed her daughters and servant. "Deborah, set the blue chamber in order; Rose, take the key of the oak press, Eleanor will help you to take out the holland sheets. Lucy, run down to old Margery, and bid her kill a couple of fowls for supper."

As the girls obeyed there entered at the front door the young officer and a soldier, supporting between them an elderly man in the dress of an officer of rank. Lady Woodley, ready of course to give her help to any person who had suffered an injury, came forward to set a chair, and at the same moment she exclaimed, in a tone of recognition, "Mr. Enderby! I am grieved to see you so much hurt."

"My Lady Woodley," he returned, recognising her at the same time, as he seated himself in the chair, "I am sorry thus to have broken in on your ladyship, but my son, Sylvester, would have me halt here."

"This gentleman is your son, then?" and a courteous greeting passed between Lady Woodley and young Sylvester Enderby, after which she again enquired after his father's accident.

"No great matter," was the reply; "a blow on the head, and a twist of the knee, that is all. Thanks to a stumbling horse, wearied out with work, I have little mind to - the pursuit of this poor young man."

"Not the King?" exclaimed Lady Woodley, breathless with alarm.

It was with no apparent satisfaction that the rebel colonel replied, "Even so, madam. Cromwell's fortune has not forsaken him; he has driven the Scots and their allies out of Worcester."

Lady Woodley was too much accustomed to evil tidings to be as much overcome by them as her young son had been; she only turned somewhat paler, and asked, "The King lives?"

"He was last seen on Worcester bridge. Troops are sent to every port whence he might attempt an escape."

"May the GOD of his father protect him," said the lady, fervently. "And my son?" she added, faintly, scarcely daring to ask the question.

"Safe, I hope," replied the colonel. "I saw him, and I could have thought him my dear old friend himself, as he joined Charles in his last desperate attempt to rally his forces, and then charged down Sidbury Street with a few bold spirits who were resolved to cover their master's retreat. He is not among the slain; he was not a prisoner when I left the headquarters. I trust he may have escaped, for Cromwell is fearfully incensed against your party."

Colonel Enderby was interrupted by Lucy's running in calling out, "Mother, mother! there are no fowls but Partlet and the sitting hen, and the old cock, and I won't have my dear old Partlet killed to be eaten by wicked Roundheads."

"Come here, my little lady," said the colonel, holding out his hand, amused by her vehemence.

"I won't speak to a Roundhead," returned Lucy, with a droll air of petulance, pleased at being courted.

Her mother spoke gravely. "You forget yourself, Lucy. This is Mr. Enderby, a friend of your dear father."

Lucy's cheeks glowed, and she looked down as she gave her hand to the colonel; but as he spoke kindly to her, her forward spirit revived, and she returned to the charge.

"You won't have Partlet killed?"

Charlotte M. Yonge

Her mother would have silenced her, but the colonel smiled and said, "No, no, little lady; I would rather go without supper than let one feather of Dame Partlet be touched."

"Nay, you need not do that either, sir," said the little chatter-box, confidentially, "for we are to have a pie made of little Jenny's pigeons; and I'll tell you what, sir, no one makes raised crust half so well as sister Rose."

Lady Woodley was not sorry to stop the current of her little girl's communications by despatching her on another message, and asking Colonel Enderby whether he would not prefer taking a little rest in his room before supper-time, offering, at the same time all the remedies for bruises and wounds that every good housekeeper of the time was sure to possess.

She had a real regard for Mr. Enderby, who had been a great friend of her husband before the unhappy divisions of the period arrayed them on opposite sides, and even then, though true friendship could not last, a kindly feeling had always existed.

Mr. Enderby was a conscientious man, but those were difficult times; and he had regarded loyalty to the King less than what he considered the rights of the people. He had been an admirer of Hampden and his principles, and had taken up arms on the same side, becoming a rebel on political, not on religious, grounds. When, as time went on, the evils of the rebellion developed themselves more fully, he was already high in command, and so involved with his own party that he had not the resolution requisite for a change of course and renunciation of his associates. He would willingly have come to terms with the King, and was earnest in the attempt at the time of the conferences at Hampden Court. He strongly disapproved of the usurpation of power by the army, and was struck with horror, grief, and dismay, at the execution of King Charles; but still he would not, or fancied that he could not, separate himself from the cause of the Parliament, and continued in their service, following Cromwell to Scotland, and fighting at Worcester on the rebel side, disliking Cromwell all the time, and with a certain inclination to the young King, and desire to see the old constitution restored.

He was just one of those men who cause such great evil by giving a sort of respectability to the wrong cause, "following a multitude to do evil," and doubtless bringing a fearful responsibility on their own heads; yet with many good qualities and excellent principles, that make those on the right side have a certain esteem for them, and grieve to see them thus perverted.

Lady Woodley, who knew him well, though sorry to have a rebel in her house at such a time, was sure that in him she had a kind and considerate guest, who would do his utmost to protect her and her children.

On his side, Colonel Enderby was much grieved and shocked at the pale, altered looks of the fair young bride he remembered, as well as the evidences of poverty throughout her house, and perhaps he had a secret wish that he was as well assured as his friend, Sir Walter, that his blood had been shed for the maintenance of the right.

CHAPTER III.

Rose Woodley ran up and down indefatigably, preparing everything for the accommodation of the guests, smoothing down Deborah's petulance, and keeping her mother from over-exertion or anxiety. Much contrivance was indeed required, for besides the colonel and his son, two soldiers had to be lodged, and four horses, which, to the consternation of old Margery, seemed likely to devour the cow's winter store of hay, while the troopers grumbled at the desolate, half-ruined, empty stables, and at the want of corn.

Rose had to look to everything; to provide blankets from the bed of the two little girls, send Eleanor to sleep with her mother, and take Lucy to her own room; despatch them on messages to the nearest cottage to borrow some eggs, and to gather vegetables in the garden, whilst she herself made the pigeon pie with the standing crust, much wishing that the soldiers were out of the way. It was a pretty thing to see her in her white apron, with her neat dexterous fingers, and nimble quiet step, doing everything in so short a time, and so well, without the least bustle.

She was at length in the hall, laying the white home-spun, home-bleached cloth, and setting the trenchers (all the Mowbray plate had long ago gone in the King's service), wondering anxiously, meantime, what could have become of Walter, with many secret and painful misgivings, though she had been striving to persuade her mother that he was only absent on some freak of his own.

Presently the door which led to the garden was opened, and to her great joy Walter put his head into the room.

"O Walter," she exclaimed, "the battle is lost! but Edmund and the King have both escaped."

"Say you so?" said Walter, smiling. "Here is a gentleman who can give you some news of Edmund."

At the same moment Rose saw her beloved eldest brother enter the room. It would be hard to say which was her first thought, joy or dismay - she had no time to ask herself. Quick as lightning she darted to the door leading to the staircase, bolted it, threw the bar across the fastening of the front entrance, and then, flying to her brother, clung fast round his neck, kissed him on each cheek, and felt his ardent kiss on her brow, as she exclaimed in a frightened whisper, "You must not stay here: there are troopers in the house!"

"Troopers! - quartered on us?" cried Walter.

Rose hastily explained, trembling lest anyone should attempt to enter. Walter paced up and down in despair, vowing that it was a trick to get a spy into the house. Edmund sat down in the large arm-chair with a calm resolute look, saying, "I must surrender, then. Neither I nor my horse can go further without rest. I will yield as a prisoner of war, and well that it is to a man of honour."

"Oh no, no!" cried Rose: "he says Cromwell treats his prisoners as rebels. It would be certain death!"

"What news of the King?" asked Edmund, anxiously.

"Not seen since the flight? but -"

"And Lord Derby, Wilmot -"

"I cannot tell, I heard no names," said Rose, "only that the enemy's cruelties are worse than ever."

Walter stood with his back against the table, gazing at his brother and sister in mute consternation.

"I know!" cried Rose, suddenly: "the out-house in the upper field. No one ever goes up into the loft but ourselves. You know, Walter, where Eleanor found the kittens. Go thither, I will bring Edmund food at night. Oh, consent, Edmund!"

"It will do! it will do!" cried Walter.

"Very well, it may spare my mother," said Edmund; and as footsteps and voices were heard on the stairs, the two brothers hurried off without another word, while Rose, trying to conceal her agitation, undid the door, and admitted her two little sisters, who were asking if they had not heard Walter's voice.

She scarcely attended to them, but, bounding upstairs to her mother's room, flung her arms round her neck, and poured into her ear her precious secret. The tremour, the joy, the fears, the tears, the throbbings of the heart, and earnest prayers, may well be imagined, crowded by the mother and daughter into those few minutes. The plan was quickly arranged. They feared to trust even Deborah; so that the only way that they could provide the food that Edmund so much needed was by Rose and Walter attempting to save all they could at supper, and Rose could steal out when everyone was gone to rest, and carry it to him. Lady Woodley was bent on herself going to her son that night; but Rose prevailed on her to lay aside the intention, as it would have been fatal, in her weak state of health, for her to expose herself to the chills of an autumn night, and, what was with her a much more conclusive reason, Rose was much more likely to be able to slip out unobserved. Rose had an opportunity of explaining all this to Walter, and imploring him to be cautious, before the colonel and his son came down, and the whole party assembled round the supper-table.

Lady Woodley had the eggs and bacon before her; Walter insisted on undertaking the carving of the pigeon-pie, and looked considerably affronted when young Sylvester Enderby offered to take the office, as a more experienced carver. Poor Rose, how her heart beat at every word and look, and how hard she strove to seem perfectly at her ease and unconscious! Walter was in a fume of anxiety and vexation, and could hardly control himself so far as to speak civilly to either of the guests, so that he was no less a cause of fear to his mother and sister than the children, who were unconscious how much depended on discretion.

Young Sylvester Enderby was a fine young man of eighteen, very good-natured, and not at all like a Puritan in appearance or manner. He had hardly yet begun to think for himself, and was merely obeying his father in joining the army with him, without questioning whether it was the right cause or not. He

Charlotte M. Yonge

was a kind elder brother at home, and here he was ready to be pleased with the children of the house. Lucy was a high-spirited talkative child, very little used to seeing strangers, and perhaps hardly reined in enough, for her poor mother's weak health had interfered with strict discipline; and as this evening Walter and Rose were both grave and serious under their anxieties, Lucy was less restrained even than usual.

She was a pretty creature, with bright blue eyes, and an arch expression, all the droller under her prim round cap; and Sylvester was a good deal amused with her pert bold little nods and airs. He paid a good deal of attention to her, and she in return grew more forward and chattering. It is what little girls will sometimes do under the pleasure and excitement of the notice of gentlemen, and it makes their friends very uneasy, since the only excuse they can have is in being VERY LITTLE, and it shows a most undesirable want of self-command and love of attention.

In addition to this feeling, Lady Woodley dreaded every word that was spoken, lest it should lead to suspicion, for though she was sure Mr. Enderby would not willingly apprehend her son, yet she could not tell what he might consider his duty to his employers; besides, there were the two soldiers to observe and report, and the discovery that Edmund was at hand might lead to frightful consequences. She tried to converse composedly with him on his family and the old neighbourhood where they had both lived, often interrupting herself to send a look or word of warning to the lower end of the table; but Lucy and Charles were too wild to see or heed her, and grew more and more unrestrained, till at last, to the dismay of her mother, brother, and sister, Charles' voice was heard so loud as to attract everyone's notice, in a shout of wonder and complaint, "Mother, mother, look! Rose has gobbled up a whole pigeon to her own share!"

Rose could not keep herself from blushing violently, as she whispered reprovingly that he must not be rude. Lucy did not mend the matter by saying with an impertinent nod, "Rose does not like to be found out."

"Children," said Lady Woodley, gravely, "I shall send you away if you do not behave discreetly."

"But, mother, Rose is greedy," said Lucy.

"Hold your tongues, little mischief makers!" burst out Walter, who had been boiling over with anxiety and indignation the whole time.

"Walter is cross now," said Lucy, pleased to have produced a sensation, and to have shocked Eleanor, who sat all the time as good, demure, and grave, as if she had been forty years old.

"Pray excuse these children," said Lady Woodley, trying to hide her anxiety under cover of displeasure at them; "no doubt Mrs. Enderby keeps much better order at home. Lucy, Charles, silence at once. Walter, is there no wine?"

"If there is, it is too good for rebels," muttered Walter to himself, as he rose. "Light me, Deborah, and I'll see."

"La! Master Walter," whispered Deborah, "you know there is nothing but the dregs of the old cask of

Charlotte M. Yonge

Malmsey, that was drunk up at the old squire's burying."

"Hush, hush, Deb," returned the boy; "fill it up with water, and it will be quite good enough for those who won't drink the King's health."

Deborah gave a half-puzzled smile. "Ye're a madcap, Master Walter! But sure, Sir, the spirit of a wolf must have possessed Mistress Rose - she that eats no supper at all, in general! D'ye think it is wearying about Master Edmund that gives her a craving?"

It might be dangerous, but Walter was so much diverted, that he could not help saying, "I have no doubt it is on his account."

"I know," said Deborah, "that I get so faint at heart that I am forced to be taking something all day long to keep about at all!"

By this time they were re-entering the hall, when there was a sound from the kitchen as of someone calling. Deborah instantly turned, screaming out joyfully, "Bless me! is it you?" and though out of sight, her voice was still heard in its high notes of joy. "You good-for-nothing rogue! are you turned up again like a bad tester, staring into the kitchen like a great oaf, as you be?"

There was a general laugh, and Eleanor said, "That must be Diggory."

"A poor country clown," said Lady Woodley, "whom we sent to join my son's troop. I hope he is in no danger."

"Oh no," said Mr. Enderby; "he has only to return to his plough."

"Hollo there!" shouted Walter. "Come in, Diggory, and show yourself."

In came Diggory, an awkward thick-set fellow, with a shock head of hair, high leathern gaiters, and a buff belt over his rough leathern jerkin. There he stood, pulling his forelock, and looking sheepish.

"Come in, Diggory," said his mistress; "I am glad to see you safe. You need not be afraid of these gentlemen. Where are the rest?"

"Slain, every man of them, an't please your ladyship."

"And your master, Mr. Woodley?"

"Down, too, an't please your ladyship."

Lucy screamed aloud; Eleanor ran to her mother, and hid her face in her lap; Charles sat staring, with great round frightened eyes. Very distressing it was to be obliged to leave the poor children in such grief and alarm, when it was plain all the time that Diggory was an arrant coward, who had fancied more deaths and dangers than were real, and was describing more than he had even thought he beheld, in order to make himself into a hero instead of a runaway. Moreover, Lady Woodley and Rose had to put on a show of grief, lest they should betray that they were better informed; and they were in agonies lest Walter's fury at the falsehoods should be as apparent to their guests as it was to themselves.

Charlotte M. Yonge

"Are you sure of what you say, Diggory?" said Lady Woodley.

"Sure as that I stand here, my lady. There was sword and shot and smoke all round. I stood it all till Farmer Ewins was cut down a-one-side of me, ma'am, and Master Edmund, more's the pity, with his brains scattered here and there on the banks of the river."

There was another cry among the children, and Walter made such a violent gesture, that Rose, covering her face with her handkerchief, whispered to him, "Walter dear, take care." Walter relieved his mind by returning, "Oh that I could cudgel the rogue soundly!"

At the same time Colonel Enderby turned to their mother, saying, "Take comfort, madam, this fellow's tale carries discredit on the face of it. Let me examine him, with your permission. Where did you last see your master?"

"I know none of your places, sir," answered Diggory, sullenly.

Colonel Enderby spoke sternly and peremptorily. "In the town, or in the fields? Answer me that, sirrah. In the field on the bank of the river?"

"Ay."

"There you left your ranks, you rogue; that was the way you lost sight of your master!" said the colonel. Then, turning to Lady Woodley, as Diggory slunk off, "Your ladyship need not be alarmed. An hour after the encounter, in which he pretends to have seen your son slain, I saw him in full health and soundness."

"A cowardly villain!" cried Walter, delighted to let out some of his indignation. "I knew he was not speaking a word of truth."

The children cheered up in a moment; but Lady Woodley was not sorry to make this agitating scene an excuse for retiring with all her children. Lucy and Eleanor were quite comforted, and convinced that Edmund must be safe; but poor little Charlie had been so dreadfully frightened by the horrors of Diggory's description, that after Rose had put him to bed he kept on starting up in his sleep, half waking, and sobbing about brother Edmund's brains.

Rose was obliged to go to him and soothe him. She longed to assure the poor little fellow that dear Edmund was perfectly safe, well, and near at hand; but the secret was too important to be trusted to one so young, so she could only coax and comfort him, and tell him they all thought it was not true, and Edmund would come back again.

"Sister," said Charlie, "may I say my prayers again for him?"

"Yes, do, dear Charlie," said Rose; "and say a prayer for King Charles too, that he may be safe from the wicked man."

So little Charlie knelt by Rose, with his hands joined, and his little bare legs folded together, and said his prayer: and did not his sister's heart go with him? Then she kissed him, covered him up warmly, and repeated to him in her soft voice the ninety-first Psalm: "Whoso dwelleth under the defence of the Most High shall abide under the shadow of the Almighty."

Charlotte M. Yonge

By the time it was ended, the little boy was fast asleep, and the faithful loyal girl felt her failing heart cheered and strengthened for whatever might be before her, sure that she, her mother, her brother, and her King, were under the shadow of the Almighty wings.

CHAPTER IV.

In a very strong fit of restlessness did little Mistress Lucy Woodley go to bed in Rose's room that night. She was quite comforted on Edmund's account, for she had discernment enough to see that her mother and sister did not believe Diggory's dreadful narration; and she had been so unsettled and excited by Mr. Sylvester Enderby's notice, and by the way in which she had allowed her high spirits to get the better of her discretion, as well as by the sudden change from terror to joy, that when first she went to Rose's room she could not attend to her prayers, and next she could not go to sleep.

Perhaps the being in a different apartment from usual, and the missing her accustomed sleeping companion, Eleanor, had something to do with it, for little Eleanor had a gravity and steadiness about her that was very apt to compose and quiet her in her idlest moods. To-night she lay broad awake, tumbling about on the very hard mattress, stuffed with chaff, wondering how Rose could bear to sleep on it, trying to guess how there could be room for both when her sister came to bed, and nevertheless in a great fidget for her to come. She listened to the howling and moaning of the wind, the creaking of the doors, and the rattling of the boards with which Rose had stopped up the broken panes of her lattice; she rolled from side to side, fancied odd shapes in the dark, and grew so restless and anxious for Rose's coming that she was just ready to jump out of bed and go in the passage to call her when Rose came into the room.

"O Rose, what a time you have been!"

It was no satisfaction to Rose to find the curious little chatter-box so wide awake at this very inconvenient time, but she did not lose her patience, and answered that she had been first with Charlie, and then with their mother.

"And now I hope you are coming to bed. I can't go to sleep without you."

"Oh, but indeed you must, Lucy dear, for I shall not be ready this long time. Look, here is a great rent in Walter's coat, which I must mend, or he won't be fit to be seen to-morrow."

"What shall we have for dinner to-morrow, Rose? What made you eat so much supper to-night?"

"I'll tell you what, Lucy, I am not going to talk to you, or you will lie awake all night, and that will be very bad for you. I shall put my candle out of your sight, and say some Psalms, but I cannot talk."

So Rose began, and, wakeful as Lucy was, she found the low sweet tones lulled her a little. But she did not like this; she had a perverse intention of staying awake till Rose got into bed, so instead of attending to the holy words, she pinched herself, and pulled herself, and kept her eyes staring open, gazing at the flickering shadows cast by the dim home-made rush candle.

She went to sleep for a moment, then started into wakefulness again; Rose had ceased to repeat her Psalms aloud, but was still at her needlework; another doze, another waking. There was some hope of Rose now, for she was kneeling down to say her prayers. Lucy thought they lasted very long, and at her next waking she was just in time to hear the latch of the door closing, and find herself left in darkness. Rose was not in bed, did not answer when she called. Oh, she must be gone to take Walter's coat back to his room. But surely she might have done that in one moment; and how long she was staying! Lucy could bear it no longer, or rather she did not try to bear it, for she was an impetuous, self-willed child, without much control over herself. She jumped out of bed, and stole to the door. A light was just disappearing on the ceiling, as if someone was carrying a candle down stairs; what could it mean? Lucy scampered, pit-pat, with her bare feet along the passage, and came to the top of the stairs in time to peep over and discover Rose silently opening the door of the hall, a large dark cloak hung over her arm, and her head and neck covered by her black silk hood and a thick woollen kerchief, as if she was going out.

Lucy's curiosity knew no bounds. She would not call, for fear she should be sent back to bed, but she was determined to see what her sister could possibly be about. Down the cold stone steps pattered she, and luckily, as she thought, Rose, probably to avoid noise, had only shut to the door, so that the little inquisitive maiden had a chink to peep through, and beheld Rose at a certain oaken corner-cupboard, whence she took out a napkin, and in it she folded what Lucy recognised as the very same three-cornered segment of pie-crust, containing the pigeon that she had last night been

Charlotte M. Yonge

accused of devouring. She placed it in a basket, and then proceeded to take a lantern from the cupboard, put in her rushlight, and, thus prepared, advanced to the garden-door, softly opened it, and disappeared.

Lucy, in an extremity of amazement, came forward. The wind howled in moaning gusts, and the rain dashed against the windows; Lucy was chilly and frightened. The fire was not out, and gave a dim light, and she crept towards the window, but a sudden terror came over her; she dashed back, looked again, heard another gust of wind, fell into another panic, rushed back to the stairs, and never stopped till she had tumbled into bed, her teeth chattering, shivering from head to foot with fright and cold, rolled herself up tight in the bed-clothes, and, after suffering excessively from terror and chill, fell sound asleep without seeing her sister return.

Causeless fears pursue those who are not in the right path, and turn from what alone can give them confidence. A sense of protection supports those who walk in innocence, though their way may seem surrounded with perils; and thus, while Lucy trembled in an agony of fright in her warm bed, Rose walked forth with a firm and fearless step through the dark gusty night, heedless of the rain that pattered round her, and the wild wind that snatched at her cloak and gown, and flapped her hood into her eyes.

She was not afraid of fancied terrors, and real perils and anxieties were at this moment lost in the bounding of her young heart at the thought of seeing, touching, speaking to her brother, her dear Edmund. She had been eleven years old when they last had parted, the morning of the battle of Naseby, and he was five years older; but they had always been very happy and fond companions and playfellows as long as she could remember, and she alone had been on anything like an equality with him, or missed him with a feeling of personal loss, that had been increased by the death of her elder sister, Mary.

Quickly, and concealing her light as much as possible, she walked down the damp ash-strewn paths of the kitchen-garden, and came out into the overgrown and neglected shrubbery, or pleasance, where the long wet-laden shoots came beating in her face, and now and then seeming to hold her back, and strange rustlings were heard that would have frightened a maiden of a less stout and earnest heart. Her anxiety was lest she should be confused by the unwonted aspect of things in the dark, and miss the path; and very, very long did it seem, while her light would only show her leaves glistening with wet. At last she gained a clearer space, the border of a field: something dark rose before her, she knew the outline of the shed, and entered the lower part. It was meant for a cart-shed, with a loft above for hay or straw; but the cart had been lost or broken, and there was only a heap of rubbish in the corner, by which the children were wont to climb up to inspect their kittens. Here Rose was for a moment startled by a glare close to her of what looked like two fiery lamps in the darkness, but the next instant a long, low, growling sound explained it, and the tabby stripes of the cat quickly darted across her lantern's range of light. She heard a slight rustling above, and ventured to call, in a low whisper, "Edmund."

"Is that you, Walter?" and as Rose proceeded to mount the pile of rubbish, his pale and haggard face looked down at her.

"What? Rose herself! I did not think you would have come on such a night as this. Can you come up? Shall I help you?"

"Thank you. Take the lantern first - take care. There. Now the basket and the cloak." And this done, with Edmund's hand, Rose scrambled up into the loft. It was only the height of the roof, and there was not room, even in the middle, to stand upright; the rain soaked through the old thatch, the floor was of rough boards, and there was but very little of the hay that had served as a bed for the kittens.

"O Edmund, this is a wretched place!" exclaimed Rose, as, crouching by his side, one hand in his, and the other round his neck, she gazed around.

"Better than a prison," he answered. "I only wish I knew that others were in as good a one. And you - why, Rose, how you are altered; you are my young lady now! And how does my dear mother?"

"Pretty well. I could hardly prevail on her not to come here to-night; but it would have been too much, she is so weak, and takes cold so soon. But, Edmund, how pale you are, how weary! Have you slept? I fear not, on these hard boards - your wound, too."

"It hardly deserves such a dignified name as a wound," said Edmund. "I am more hungry than aught else; I could have slept but for hunger, and now" - as he spoke he was opening the basket - "I shall be lodged better, I fear, than a king, with that famous cloak. What a notable piece of pasty! Well done, Rose! Are you housewife? Store of candles, too. This is noble!"

"How hungry you must be! How long is it since you have eaten?"

"Grey sent his servant into a village to buy some bread and cheese; we divided it when we parted, and it lasted me until this morning. Since then I have fasted."

"Dear brother, I wish I could do more for you; but till Mr. Enderby goes, I cannot, for the soldiers are about the kitchen, and our maid, Deborah, talks too much to be trustworthy, though she is thoroughly faithful."

"This is excellent fare," said Edmund, eating with great relish. "And now tell me of yourselves. My mother is feeble and unwell, you say?"

"Never strong, but tolerably well at present."

"So Walter said. By the way, Walter is a fine spirited fellow. I should like to have him with me if we take another African voyage."

"He would like nothing better, poor fellow. But what strange things you have seen and done since we met! How little we thought that morning that it would be six years before we should sit side by side again! And Prince Rupert is kind to you?"

"He treats me like a son or brother: never was man kinder," said Edmund, warmly. "But the children? I must see them before I depart. Little Lucy, is she as bold and pert as she was as a young child?"

"Little changed," said Rose, smiling, and telling her brother the adventures at the dinner.

As cheerfully as might be they talked till Edmund had finished his meal, and then Rose begged him to let her examine and bind up the wound. It was a sword-cut on the right shoulder, and, though not very deep, had become stiff and painful from neglect, and had soaked his sleeve deeply with blood. Rose's dexterous fingers applied the salve and linen she had brought, and she promised that at her next visit she would bring him some clean clothes, which was what he said he most wished for. Then she arranged the large horseman's cloak, the hay, and his own mantle, so well as to form, he said, the most luxurious resting place he had seen since he left Dunbar; and rolled up in this he lay, his head supported on his hand, talking earnestly with her on the measures next to be taken for his safety, and on the state of the family. He must be hidden there till the chase was a little slackened, and then escape, by Bosham or some other port, to the royal fleet, which was hovering on the coast. Money, however - how was he to get a passage without it?

"The Prince, at parting - heaven knows he has little enough himself - gave me twenty gold crowns, which he said was my share of prize-money for our captures," said Edmund, "but this is the last of them."

"And I don't know how we can get any," said Rose. "We never see money. Our tenants, if they pay at all, pay in kind - a side of bacon, or a sack of corn; they are very good, poor people, and love our mother heartily, I do believe. I wish I knew what was to be done."

"Time will show," said Edmund. "I have been in as bad a case as this ere now, and it is something to be near you al again. So you like this place, do you? As well as our own home?"

Rose shook her head, and tears sprang into her eyes. "Oh no, Edmund; I try to think it home, and the children feel it so, but it is not like Woodley. Do you remember the dear old oak-tree, with the branches that came down so low, where you used to swing Mary and me?"

"And the high branch where I used to watch for my father coming home from the justice-meeting. And the meadow where the hounds killed the fox that had baffled them so long! Do you hear anything of the place now, Rose?"

"Mr. Enderby told us something," said Rose, sadly. "You know who has got it, Edmund?"

"Who?

"That Master Priggins, who was once justices' clerk."

"Ha!" cried Edmund. "That pettifogging scrivener in my father's house! - in my ancestors' house! A rogue that ought to have been branded a dozen years ago! I could have stood anything but that! Pretty work he is making there, I suppose! Go on, Rose."

"O Edmund, you know it is but what the King himself has to bear."

"Neighbour's fare! as you say," replied Edmund, with a short dry laugh. "Poverty and wandering I could bear; peril is what any brave man naturally seeks; the acres that have been ours for centuries could not go in a better cause; but to hear of a rascal such as that in my father's place is enough to drive one mad with rage! Come, what has he been doing? How has he used the poor people?"

"He turned out old Davy and Madge at once from keeping the house, but Mr. Enderby took them in, and gave them a cottage."

"I wonder what unlucky fate possessed that Enderby to take the wrong side! Well?"

"He could not tell us much of the place, for he cannot endure Master Priggins, and Master Sylvester laughs at his Puritanical manner; but he says - O Edmund - that the fish-ponds are filled up - those dear old fish-ponds where the water-lilies used to blow, and you once pulled me out of the water."

"Ay, ay! we shall not know it again if ever our turn comes, and we enjoy our own again. But it is of no use to think about such matters."

"No; we must be thankful that we have a home at all, and are not like so many, who are actually come to beggary, like poor Mrs. Forde. You remember her, our old clergyman's widow. He died on board ship, and she was sent for by her cousin, who promised her a home; but she had no money, and was forced to walk all the way, with her two little boys, getting a lodging at night from any loyal family who would shelter her for the love of heaven. My mother wept when she saw how sadly she was changed; we kept her with us a week to rest her, and when she went she had our last gold carolus, little guessing, poor soul, that it was our last. Then, when she was gone, my mother called us all round her, and gave thanks that she could still give us shelter and daily bread."

"There is a Judge above!" exclaimed Edmund; "yet sometimes it is hard to believe, when we see such a state of things here below!"

"Dr. Bathurst tells us to think it will all be right in the other world, even if we do have to see the evil prosper here," said Rose, gravely. "The sufferings will all turn to glory, just as they did with our blessed King, out of sight."

Edmund sat thoughtful. "If our people abroad would but hope and trust and bear as you do here, Rose. But I had best not talk of these things, only your patience makes me feel how deficient in it we are, who have not a tithe to bear of what you have at home. Are you moving to go? Must you?"

"I fear so, dear brother; the light seems to be beginning to dawn, and if Lucy wakes and misses me - Is your shoulder comfortable?"

"I was never more comfortable in my life. My loving duty to my dear mother. Farewell, you, sweet Rose."

"Farewell, dear Edmund. Perhaps Walter may manage to visit you, but do not reckon on it."

Charlotte M. Yonge

CHAPTER V.

The vigils of the night had been as unwonted for Lucy as for her sister, and she slept soundly till Rose was already up and dressed. Her first reflection was on the strange sights she had seen, followed by a doubt whether they were real, or only a dream; but she was certain it was no such thing; she recollected too well the chill of the stone to her feet, and the sound of the blasts of wind. She wondered over it, wished to make out the cause, but decided that she should only be scolded for peeping, and she had better keep her own counsel.

That Lucy should keep silence when she thought she knew more than other people was, however, by no means to be expected; and though she would say not a word to her mother or Rose, of whom she was afraid, she was quite ready to make the most of her knowledge with Eleanor.

When she came down stairs she found Walter, with his elbows on the table and his book before him, learning the task which his mother required of him every day; Eleanor had just come in with her lapfull of the still lingering flowers, and called her to help to make them up into nosegays.

Lucy came and sat down by her on the floor, but paid

little attention to the flowers, so intent was she on showing her knowledge.

"Ah! you don't know what I have seen."

"I dare say it is only some nonsense," said Eleanor, gravely, for she was rather apt to plume herself on being steadier than her elder sister.

"It is no nonsense," said Lucy. "I know what I know."

Before Eleanor had time to answer this speech, the mystery of which was enhanced by a knowing little nod of the head, young Mr. Enderby made his appearance in the hall, with a civil good-morning to Walter, which the boy hardly deigned to acknowledge by a gruff reply and little nod, and then going on to the little girls, renewed with them yesterday's war of words. "Weaving posies, little ladies?"

"Not for rebels," replied Lucy, pertly.

"May I not have one poor daisy?"

"Not one; the daisy is a royal flower."

"If I take one?"

"Rebels take what they can't get fairly," said Lucy, with the smartness of a forward child; and Sylvester, laughing heartily, continued, "What would General Cromwell say to such a nest of little malignants?"

"That is an ugly name," said Eleanor.

"Quite as pretty as Roundhead."

"Yes, but we don't deserve it."

"Not when you make that pretty face so sour?"

"Ah!" interposed Lucy, "she is sour because I won't tell her my secret of the pie."

"Oh, what?" said Eleanor.

"Now I have you!" cried Lucy, delighted. "I know what became of the pigeon pie."

In extreme alarm and anger, Walter turned round as he caught these words. "Lucy, naughty child!" he began, in a voice of thunder; then, recollecting the danger of exciting further suspicion, he stammered, "what - what - what - are you doing here? Go along to mother."

Lucy rubbed her fingers into her eyes, and answered sharply, in a pettish tone, that she was doing no harm. Eleanor, in amazement, asked what could be the matter.

"Intolerable!" exclaimed Walter. "So many girls always in the way?"

Sylvester Enderby could not help smiling, as he asked, "Is that all you have to complain of?"

"I could complain of something much worse," muttered Walter. "Get away, Lucy?"

"I won't at your bidding, sir."

To Walter's great relief, Rose entered at that moment, and all was smooth and quiet; Lucy became silent, and the conversation was kept up in safe terms between Rose and the young officer. The colonel, it appeared, was so much better that he intended to leave Forest Lea that very day; and it was not long before he came down, and presently afterwards Lady Woodley, looking very pale and exhausted, for her anxieties had kept her awake all night.

After a breakfast on bread, cheese, rashers of bacon, and beer, the horses were brought to the door, and the colonel took his leave of Lady Woodley, thanking her much for her hospitality.

"I wish it had been better worth accepting," said she.

"I wish it had, though not for my own sake," said the colonel. "I wish you would allow me to attempt something in your favour. One thing, perhaps, you will deign to accept. Every royalist house, especially those belonging to persons engaged at Worcester, is liable to be searched, and to have soldiers quartered on them, to prevent fugitives from being harboured there. I will send Sylvester at once to obtain a protection for you, which may prevent you from being thus disturbed."

"That will be a kindness, indeed," said Lady Woodley, hardly able to restrain the eagerness with which she heard the offer made, that gave the best hope of saving her son. She was not certain that the colonel had not some suspicion of the true state of the case, and would not take notice, unwilling to ruin the son of his friend, and at the same time reluctant to fail in his duty to his employers.

He soon departed; Mistress Lucy's farewell to Sylvester being thus: "Good-bye, Mr. Roundhead, rebel, crop-eared traitor." At which Sylvester and his father turned and laughed, and their two soldiers looked very much astonished.

Lady Woodley called Lucy at once, and spoke to her seriously on her forwardness and impertinence. "I could tell you, Lucy, that it is not like a young lady, but I must tell you more, it is not like a young Christian maiden. Do you remember the text that I gave you to learn a little while ago - the ornament fit for a woman?"

Lucy hung her head, and with tears filling her eyes, as her mother prompted her continually, repeated the text in a low mumbling voice, half crying: "Whose adorning, let it not be the putting on of gold, or the plaiting of hair, or the putting on of apparel, but let it be the hidden man of the heart, even the ornament of a meek and quiet spirit, which is in the sight of GOD of great price."

"And does my little Lucy think she showed that ornament when she pushed herself forward to talk idle nonsense, and make herself be looked at and taken notice of?"

Lucy put her finger in her mouth; she did not like to be scolded, as she called it, gentle as her mother was, and she would not open her mind to take in the kind reproof.

Lady Woodley took the old black-covered Bible, and finding two of the verses in S. James about the government of the tongue, desired Lucy to learn them by heart before she went out of the house; and the little girl sat down with them in the window-seat, in a cross impatient mood, very unfit for learning those sacred words. "She had done no harm," she thought; "she could not help it if the young gentleman would talk to her!"

So there she sat, with the Bible in her lap, alone, for Lady Woodley was so harassed and unwell, in consequence of her anxieties, that Rose had persuaded her to go and lie down on her bed, since it would be better for her not to try to see Edmund till the promised protection had arrived, lest suspicion should be excited. Rose was busy about her household affairs; Eleanor, a handy little person, was helping her; and Walter and Charles were gone out to gather apples for a pudding which she had promised them.

Lucy much wished to be with them; and after a long brooding over her ill-temper, it began to wear out, not to be conquered, but to depart of itself; she thought she might as well learn her lesson and have done with it; so by way of getting rid of the task, not of profiting by the warning it conveyed, she hurried through the two verses ending with - "Behold how great a matter a little fire kindleth!"

As soon as she could say them perfectly, she raced upstairs, and into her mother's room, gave her the book, and repeated them at her fastest pace. Poor Lady Woodley was too weary and languid to exert herself to speak to the little girl about her unsuitable manner, or to try to bring the lesson home to her; she dismissed her, only saying, "I hope, my dear, you will remember this," and away ran Lucy, first to the orchard in search of her brothers, and not finding them there, round and round the garden and pleasance. Edmund, in his hiding-place, heard the voice calling "Walter!

Charlie!" and peeping out, caught a glimpse of a little figure, her long frock tucked over her arm, and long locks of dark hair blowing out from under her small, round, white cap. What a pleasure it was to him to have that one view of his little sister!

At last, tired with her search, Lucy returned to the house, and there found Deborah ironing at the long table in the hall, and crooning away her one dismal song of "Barbara Allen's cruelty."

"So you can sing again, Deb," she began, "now the Roundheads are gone and Diggory come back?"

"Little girls should not meddle with what does not concern them," answered Deborah.

"You need not call me a little girl," said Lucy. "I am almost eleven years old; and I know a secret, a real secret."

"A secret, Mistress Lucy? Who would tell their secrets to the like of you?" said Deborah, contemptuously.

"No one told me; I found it out for myself!" cried Lucy, in high exultation. "I know what became of the pigeon pie that we thought Rose ate up!"

"Eh? Mistress Lucy!" exclaimed Deborah, pausing in her ironing, full of curiosity.

Lucy was delighted to detail the whole of what she had observed.

"Well!" cried Deborah, "if ever I heard tell the like! That slip of a thing out in all the blackness of the night! I should be afraid of my life of the ghosts and hobgoblins. Oh! I had rather be set up for a mark for all the musketeers in the Parliament army, than set one foot out of doors after dark!"

As Deborah spoke, Walter came into the hall. He saw that Lucy had observed something, and was anxious every time she opened her lips. This made him rough and sharp with her, and he instantly exclaimed, "How now, Lucy, still gossipping?"

"You are so cross, I can't speak a word for you," said Lucy, fretfully, walking out of the room, while Walter, in his usual imperious way, began to shout for Diggory and his boots. "Diggory, knave!"

"Anon, sir!" answered the dogged voice.

"Bring them, I say, you laggard!"

"Coming, sir, coming."

"Coming, are you, you snail?" cried Walter, impatiently. "Your heels are tardier now than they were at Worcester!"

"A man can't do more nor he can do, sir," said Diggory, sullenly, as he plodded into the hall.

"Answering again, lubber?" said Walter. "Is this what you call cleaned? You are not fit for your own shoe-blacking trade! Get along with you!" and he threw the boots at Diggory in a passion. "I must wear them, though, as they are, or wait all day. Bring them to me again."

Walter had some idle notion in his head that it was Puritanical to speak courteously to servants, and despising Diggory for his cowardice and stupidity, he was especially overbearing with him, and went on rating him all the time he was putting on his boots, to go out and try to catch some fish for the morrow's dinner, which was likely to be but scanty. As soon as he was gone, Diggory, who had listened in sulky silence, began to utter his complaints.

"Chicken-heart, moon-calf, awkward lubber, those be the best words a poor fellow gets. I can tell Master Walter that these are no times for gentlefolks to be hectoring, especially when they haven't a penny to pay wages with."

"You learnt that in the wars, Diggory," said Deborah, turning round, for, grumble as she might herself, she could not bear to have a word said by anyone else against her lady's family, and loved to scold her sweetheart, Diggory. "Never mind Master Walter. If he has not a penny in his pocket, and the very green coat to his back is cut out of his grandmother's farthingale, more's the pity. How should he show he is a gentleman but by hectoring a bit now and then, 'specially to such a rogue as thou, coming back when thy betters are lost. That is always the way, as I found when I lost my real silver crown, and kept my trumpery Parliament bit."

"Ah, Deb!" pleaded Diggory, "thou knowst not what danger is! I thought thou wouldst never have set eyes on poor Diggory again."

"Much harm would that have been," retorted Mrs. Deb, tossing her head. "D'ye think I'd have broke my heart? That I'll never do for a runaway."

"'Twas time to run when poor Farmer Ewins was cut down, holloaing for quarter, and Master Edmund's brains lying strewn about on the ground, for all the world like a calf's."

"'Tis your own brains be like a calf's," said Deborah. "I'd bargain to eat all of Master Edmund's brains you ever saw."

"He's as dead as a red herring."

"I say he is as life-like as you or I."

"I say I saw him stretched out, covered with blood, and a sword-cut on his head big enough to be the death of twenty men."

"Didn't that colonel man, as they call him, see him alive and merry long after? It's my belief that Master Edmund is not a dozen miles off."

"Master Edmund! hey, Deb? I'll never believe that, after what I've seen at Worcester."

"Then pray why does Mistress Rose save a whole pigeon out of the pie, hide it in her lap, and steal out of the house with it at midnight? Either Master Edmund is in hiding, or some other poor gentleman from the wars, and I verily believe it is Master Edmund himself; so a fig for his brains or yours, and there's for you, for a false-tongued runaway! Coming, mistress, coming!" and away ran Deborah at a call from Rose.

Now Deborah was faithful to the backbone, and would have given all she had in the world, almost her life itself, for her lady and the children; she was a good and honest woman in the main, but tongue and temper were two things that she had never learnt to restrain, and she had given her love to the first person by whom it was sought, without consideration whether he was worthy of affection or not. That Diggory was a sullen, ill-conditioned, selfish fellow, was evident to everyone else; but he had paid court to Deborah, and therefore the foolish woman had allowed herself to be taken with him, see perfections in him, promise to become his wife, and confide in him.

When Deborah left the hall, Diggory returned to his former employment of chopping wood, and began to consider very intently for him.

He had really believed, at the moment of his panic-terror, that he saw Edmund Woodley fall, and had at once taken flight, without attempting to afford him any assistance. The story of the brains had, of course, been invented on the spur of the moment, by way of excusing his flight, and he was obliged to persist in the falsehood he had once uttered, though he was not by any means certain that it had been his master whom he saw killed, especially after hearing Colonel Enderby's testimony. And now there came alluringly before him the promise of the reward offered for the discovery of the fugitive cavaliers, the idea of being able to rent and stock poor Ewins's farm, and setting up there with Deborah. It was money easily come by, he thought, and he would like to be revenged on Master Walter, and show him that the lubber and moon-calf could do some harm, after all. A relenting came across him as he thought of his lady and Mistress Rose, though he had no personal regard for Edmund, who had never lived at Forest Lea; and his stolid mind was too much enclosed in selfishness to admit much feeling for anyone. Besides, it might not be Master Edmund; he was probably killed; it might be one of the lords in the battle, or even the King himself, and that would be worth 1,000 pounds. Master Cantwell called them all tyrants and sons of Belial, and what not; and though Dr. Bathurst said differently, who was to know what was right? Dr. Bathurst had had his day, and this was Cantwell's turn. There was a comedown now of feathered hats, and point collars, and curled hair; and leathern jerkin should have its day. And as for being an informer, he would keep his own counsel; at any rate, the reward he would have. It was scarcely likely to be a hanging matter, after all; and if the gentleman, whoever he might be, did chance to be taken, he would get off scot free, no harm done to him. "Diggory Stokes, you're a made man!" he finished, throwing his bill-hook from him.

Ah! Lucy, Lucy, you little thought of the harm your curiosity and chattering had done, as you saw Diggory stealing along the side of the wood, in the direction leading to Chichester!

CHAPTER VI.

In the afternoon Lady Woodley was so much better as to be able to come downstairs, and all the party sat round the fire in the twilight. Walter was just come in from his fishing, bringing a basket of fine trout; Eleanor and Charles were admiring their beautiful red spots, Lucy wondering what made him so late, while he cast a significant look at his eldest sister, showing her that he had been making a visit to Edmund.

At that moment a loud authoritative knocking was heard at the door; Walter shouted to Diggory to open it, and was answered by Deborah's shrill scream from the kitchen, "He's not here, sir; I've not seen him since you threw your boots at him, sir."

Another thundering knock brought Deborah to open the door; and what was the dismay of the mother and children as there entered six tall men, their buff coats, steeple-crowned hats, plain collars, and thick calf-skin boots, marking them as Parliamentary soldiers. With a shriek of terror the little ones clung round their mother, while he who, by his orange scarf, was evidently the commanding officer, standing in the middle of the hall, with his hat on, announced, in a Puritanical tone, "We are here by order of his Excellency, General Cromwell, to search for and apprehend the body of the desperate malignant Edmund Woodley, last seen in arms against the Most High Court of Parliament. Likewise to arrest the person of Dame Mary Woodley, widow, suspected of harbouring and concealing traitors:" and he advanced to lay his hand upon her. Walter, in an impulse of passion, rushed forward, and aimed a blow at him with the butt-end of the fishing-rod; but it was the work of a moment to seize the boy and tie his hands, while his mother earnestly implored the soldier to have pity on him, and excuse his thoughtless haste to protect her.

The officer sat down in the arm-chair, and without replying to Lady Woodley, ordered a soldier to bring the boy before him, and spoke thus:- "Hear me, son of an ungodly seed. So merciful are the lessons of the light that thou contemnest, that I will even yet over-look and forgive the violence wherewith thou didst threaten my life, so thou wilt turn again, and confess where thou hast hidden the bloody-minded traitor."

"This house harbours no traitor," answered Walter, undauntedly.

"If thou art too hardened to confess," continued the officer, frowning, and speaking slowly and sternly, as he kept his eyes steadily fixed on Walter, "if thou wilt not reveal his hiding-place, I lead thee hence to abide the penalty of attempted murder."

"I am quite ready," answered Walter, returning frown for frown, and not betraying how his heart throbbed.

The officer signed to the soldier, who roughly dragged him aside by the cord that tied his hands, cutting them severely, though he disdained to show any sign of pain.

Charlotte M. Yonge

"Young maiden," continued the rebel, turning to Rose, "what sayest thou? Wilt thou see thy brother led away to death, when the breath of thy mouth might save him?"

Poor Rose turned as pale as death, but her answer was steady: "I will say nothing."

"Little ones, then," said the officer, fiercely, "speak, or you shall taste the rod. Do you know where your brother is?"

"No - no," sobbed Lucy; and her mother added, "They know nothing, sir."

"It is loss of time to stand parleying with women and children," said the officer, rising. "Here," to one of his men, "keep the door. Let none quit the chamber, and mark the children's talk. The rest with me. Where is the fellow that brought the tidings?"

Diggory, who had slunk out of sight, was pushed forward by two of the soldiers, and at the same time there was a loud scream from Deborah. "Oh! Diggory, is it you? Oh! my Lady, my Lady, forgive me! I meant no harm! Oh! who would have thought it?" And in an agony of distress, she threw her apron over her face, and, sinking on the bench, rocked herself to and fro, sobbing violently.

In the meantime, the officer and his men, all but the sentinel, had left the room to search for the fugitive, leaving Lady Woodley sitting exhausted and terrified in her chair, the little ones clinging around her, Walter standing opposite, with his hands bound; Rose stood by him, her arm round his neck, proud of his firmness, but in dreadful terror for him, and in such suspense for Edmund, that her whole being seemed absorbed in agonised prayer. Deborah's sobs, and the children's frightened weeping, were all the sounds that could be heard; Rose was obliged to attempt to soothe them, but her first kind word to Deborah produced a fresh burst of violent weeping, and then a loud lamentation: "Oh! the rogue - the rogue. If I could have dreamt it!"

"What has she done?" exclaimed Walter, impatiently. "Come, stop your crying. What have you done, Deb?"

"I thought - Oh! if I had known what was in the villain!" continued Deborah, "I'd sooner have bit out my tongue than have said one word to him about the pigeon pie."

"Pigeon pie!" repeated Rose.

Lucy now gave a cry, for she was, with all her faults, a truth-telling child. "Mother! mother! I told Deb about the pigeon pie! Oh, what have I done? Was it for Edmund? Is Edmund here?"

And to increase the danger and perplexity, the other two children exclaimed together, "Is Edmund here?"

"Hush, hush, my dears, be quiet; I cannot answer you now," whispered Lady Woodley, trying to silence them by caresses, and looking with terror at the rigid, stern guard, who, instead of remaining at the door where he had been posted, had come close up to them, and sat himself down at the end of the table, as if to catch every word they uttered.

Eleanor and Charles obeyed their mother's command

that they should be silent; Rose took Lucy on her lap, let her rest her head on her shoulder, and whispered to her that she should hear and tell all another time, but she must be quiet now, and listen. Deborah kept her apron over her face, and Walter, leaning his shoulder against the wall, stood gazing at them all; and while he was intently watching for every sound that could enable him to judge whether the search was successful or not, at the same time his heart was beating and his head swimming at the threat of the rebel. Was he to die? To be taken away from that bright world, from sunshine, youth, and health, from his mother, and all of them, and be laid, a stiff mangled corpse, in some cold, dark, unregarded grave; his pulses, that beat so fast, all still and silent - senseless, motionless, like the birds he had killed? And that was not all: that other world! To enter on what would last for ever and ever and ever, on a state which he had never dwelt on or realised to himself, filled him with a blank, shuddering awe; and next came a worse, a sickening thought: if his feeling for the bliss of heaven was almost distaste, could he be fit for it? could he dare to hope for it? It was his Judge Whom he was about to meet, and he had been impatient and weary of Bible and Catechism, and Dr. Bathurst's teaching; he had been inattentive and careless at his prayers; he had been disobedient and unruly, violent, and unkind! Such a horror and agony came over the poor boy, so exceeding a dread of death, that he was ready at that moment to struggle to do anything to save himself; but there came the recollection that the price of his rescue must be the betrayal of Edmund. He would almost have spoken at that instant; the next he sickened at the thought. Never, never - he could not, would not; better not live at all than be a traitor! He was too confused and anxious to pray, for he had not taught himself to fix his attention in quiet moments. He would not speak before the rebel soldier; but only looked with an earnest gaze at his sister, who, as their eyes met, understood all it conveyed.

His mother, after the first moment's fright, had reassured herself somewhat on his account; he was so mere a boy that it was not likely that Algernon Sydney, who then commanded at Chichester, would put him to death; a short imprisonment was the worst that was likely to befall him; and though that was enough to fill her with terror and anxiety, it could at that moment be scarcely regarded in comparison with her fears for her eldest son.

A long time passed away, so long, that they began to hope that the enemies might be baffled in their search, in spite of Diggory's intimate knowledge of every nook and corner. They had been once to the shrubbery, and had been heard tramping back to the stable, where they were welcome to search as long as they chose, then to the barn-yard, all over the house from garret to cellar. Was it over? Joy! joy! But the feet were heard turning back to the pleasance, as though to recommence the search, and ten minutes after the steps came nearer. The rebel officer entered the hall first, but, alas! behind him came, guarded by two soldiers, Edmund Woodley himself, his step firm, his head erect, and his hands unbound. His mother sank back in her chair, and he, going straight up to her, knelt on one knee before her, saying, "Mother, dear mother, your blessing. Let me see your face again."

She threw her arms round his neck, "My son! and is it thus we meet?"

Charlotte M. Yonge

"We only meet as we parted," he answered firmly and cheerfully. "Still sufferers in the same good cause; still, I trust, with the same willing hearts."

"Come, sir," said the officer, "I must see you safely bestowed for the night."

"One moment, gentlemen," entreated Lady Woodley. "It is six years since I saw my son, and this may be our last meeting." She led him to the light, and looked earnestly up into his face, saying, with a smile, which had in it much of pride and pleasure, as well as sadness, "How you are altered, Edmund! See, Rose, how brown he is, and how much darker his hair has grown; and does not his moustache make him just like your father?"

"And my little sisters," said Edmund. "Ha! Lucy, I know your little round face."

"Oh," sobbed Lucy, "is it my fault? Can you pardon me? The pigeon pie!"

"What does she mean?" asked Edmund, turning to Rose.

"I saw you take it out at night, Rose," said poor Lucy. "I told Deb!"

"And poor Deborah," added Rose, "from the same thoughtlessness repeated her chatter to Diggory, who has betrayed us."

"The cowardly villain," cried Walter, who had come forward to the group round his brother.

"Hush, Walter," said Edmund. "But what do I see? Your hands bound? You a prisoner?"

"Poor Walter was rash enough to attempt resistance," said his mother.

"So, sir," said Edmund, turning to the rebel captain, "you attach great importance to the struggles of a boy of thirteen!"

"A blow with the butt-end of a fishing-rod is no joke from boy or man," answered the officer.

"When last I served in England," continued the cavalier, "Cromwell's Ironsides did not take notice of children with fishing-rods. You can have no warrant, no order, or whatever you pretend to act by, against him."

"Why - no, sir; but - however, the young gentleman has had a lesson, and I do not care if I do loose his hands. Here, unfasten him. But I cannot permit him to be at large while you are in the house."

"Very well, then, perhaps you will allow him to share my chamber. We have been separated for so many years, and it may be our last meeting."

"So let it be. Since you are pleased to be conformable, sir, I am willing to oblige you," answered the rebel, whose whole demeanour had curiously changed in the presence of one of such soldierly and gentleman-like bearing as Edmund, prisoner though he was. "Now, madam, to your own chamber. You will all meet to-morrow."

Charlotte M. Yonge

"Good-night, mother," said Edmund. "Sleep well; think this is but a dream, and only remember that your eldest son is in your own house."

"Good-night, my brave boy," said Lady Woodley, as she embraced him ardently. "A comfort, indeed, I have in knowing that with your father's face you have his steadfast, loving, unselfish heart. We meet to-morrow. GOD'S blessing be upon you, my boy."

And tenderly embracing the children she left the hall, followed by a soldier, who was to guard her door, and allow no one to enter. Edmund next kissed his sisters and little Charles, affectionately wishing them good-night, and assuring the sobbing Lucy of his pardon. Rose whispered to him to say something to comfort Deborah, who continued to weep piteously.

"Deborah," he said, "I must thank you for your long faithful service to my mother in her poverty and distress. I am sure you knew not that you were doing me any harm."

"Oh, sir," cried poor Deborah, "Oh don't speak so kind! I had rather stand up to be a mark for all the musketeers in the Parliament army than be where I am now."

Edmund did not hear half what she said, for he and Walter were obliged to hasten upstairs to the chamber which was to be their prison for the night. Rose, at the same time, led away the children, poor little Charles almost asleep in the midst of the confusion.

Deborah's troubles were not over yet; the captain called for supper, and seeing Walter's basket of fish, ordered her to prepare them at once for him. Afraid to refuse, she took them down to the kitchen, and proceeded to her cookery, weeping and lamenting all the time.

"Oh, the sweet generous-hearted young gentleman! That I should have been the death of such as he, and he thanking me for my poor services! 'Tis little I could do, with my crooked temper, that plagues all I love the very best, and my long tongue! Oh that it had been bitten out at the root! I wish - I wish I was a mark for all the musketeers in the Parliament army this minute! And Diggory, the rogue! Oh, after having known him all my life, who would have thought of his turning informer? Why was not he killed in the great fight? It would have broke my heart less."

And having set her fish to boil, Deborah sank on the chair, her apron over her head, and proceeded to rock herself backwards and forwards as before. She was startled by a touch, and a lumpish voice, attempted to be softened into an insinuating tone. "I say, Deb, don't take on."

She sprung up as if an adder had stung her, and jumped away from him. "Ha! is it you? Dost dare to speak to an honest girl?"

"Come, come, don't be fractious, my pretty one," said Diggory, in the amiable tones that had once gained her heart.

But now her retort was in a still sharper, more angry key. "Your'n, indeed! I'd rather stand up to be a mark for all the musketeers in the Parliament army, as poor Master Edmund is like to be, all along of you. O

Diggory Stokes," she added ruefully, "I'd not have believed it of you, if my own father had sworn it."

"Hush, hush, Deb!" said Diggory, rather sheepishly, "they've done hanging the folk."

"Don't be for putting me off with such trash," she returned, more passionately; "you've murdered him as much as if you had cut his throat, and pretty nigh Master Walter into the bargain; and you've broke my lady's heart, you, as was born on her land and fed with her bread. And now you think to make up to me, do you?"

"Wasn't it all along of you I did it? For your sake?"

"Well, and what would you be pleased to say next?" cried Deb, her voice rising in shrillness with her indignation.

"Patience, Deb," said Diggory, showing a heavy leathern bag. "No more toiling in this ruinous old hall, with scanty scraps, hard words, and no wages; but a tidy little homestead, pig, cow, and horse, your own. See here, Deb," and he held up a piece of money.

"Silver!" she exclaimed.

"Ay, ay," said Diggory, grinning, and jingling the bag, "and there be plenty more where that came from."

"It is the price of Master Edmund's blood."

"Don't ye say that now, Deb; 'tis all for you!" he answered, thinking he was prevailing because she was less violent, too stupid to perceive the difference between her real indignation and perpetual scolding.

"So you still have the face to tell me so!" she burst out, still more vehemently. "I tell you, I'd rather serve my lady and Mistress Rose, if they had not a crust to give me, than roll in gold with a rogue like you. Get along with you, and best get out of the county, for not a boy in Dorset but will cry shame on you."

"But Deb, Deb," he still pleaded.

"You will have it, then!" And dealing him a hearty box on the ear, away ran Deborah. Down fell bag, money, and all, and Diggory stood gaping and astounded for a moment, then proceeded to grope after the coins on his hands and knees.

Suddenly a voice exclaimed, "How now, knave, stealing thy mistress's goods?" and a tall, grim, steeple-hatted figure, armed with a formidable halberd, stood over him.

"Good master corporal," he began, trembling; but the soldier would not hear him.

"Away with thee, son of iniquity or I will straightway lay mine halberd about thine ears. I bethink me that I saw thee at the fight of Worcester, on the part of the man Charles Stuart." Here Diggory judged it prudent to slink away through the back door. "And so," continued the Puritan corporal, as he swept the silver into his pouch, "and so the gains of iniquity fall into the hands of the righteous!"

In the meantime Edmund and Walter had been conducted up stairs to Walter's bed-room, and there locked in, a sentinel standing outside the door. No sooner were they there than Walter swung himself round with a gesture of rage and despair. "The villains! the rogues! To be betrayed by such a wretch, who has eaten our bread all his life. O Edmund, Edmund!"

"It is a most unusual, as well as an unhappy chance," returned Edmund. "Hitherto it has generally happened that servants have given remarkable proofs of fidelity. Of course this fellow can have no attachment for me; but I should have thought my mother's gentle kindness must have won the love of all who came near her, both for herself and all belonging to her."

A recollection crossed Walter: he stood for a few moments in silence, then suddenly exclaimed, "The surly rascal! I verily believe it was all spite at me, for -"

"For - " repeated Edmund.

"For rating him as he deserved," answered Walter. "I wish I had given it to him more soundly, traitor as he is. No, no, after all," added he, hesitating, "perhaps if I had been civiller -"

"I should guess you to be a little too prompt of tongue," said Edmund, smiling.

"It is what my mother is always blaming me for," said Walter; "but really, now, Edmund, doesn't it savour of the crop-ear to be picking one's words to every rogue in one's way?"

"Nay, Walter, you should not ask me that question, just coming from France. There we hold that the best token, in our poverty, that we are cavaliers and gentlemen, is to be courteous to all, high and low. You should see our young King's frank bright courtesy; and as to the little King Louis, he is the very pink of civility to every old poissarde in the streets."

Walter coloured a little, and looked confused; then repeated, as if consoling himself, "He is a sullen, spiteful, good-for-nothing rogue, whom hanging is too good for."

"Don't let us spend our whole night in abusing him," said Edmund; "I want to make the most of you, Walter, for this our last sight of each other."

"O, Edmund! you don't mean - they shall not - you shall escape. Oh! is there no way out of this room?" cried Walter, running round it like one distracted, and bouncing against the wainscot, as if he would shake it down.

"Hush! this is of no use, Walter," said his brother. "The window is, I see, too high from the ground, and there is no escape."

Walter stood regarding him with blank dismay.

"For one thing I am thankful to them," continued Edmund; "I thought they might have shot me down before my mother's door, and so filled the place with horror for her ever after. Now they have given me time for preparation, and she will grow accustomed to the thought of losing me."

"Then you think there is no hope? O Edmund!"

"I see none. Sydney is unlikely to spare a friend of Prince Rupert's."

Walter squeezed his hands fast together. "And how - how can you? Don't think me cowardly, Edmund, for that I will never be; never -"

"Never, I am sure," repeated Edmund.

"But when that base Puritan threatened me just now - perhaps it was foolish to believe him - I could answer him freely enough; but when I thought of dying, then -"

"You have not stood face to face with death so often as I have, Walter," said Edmund; "nor have you led so wandering and weary a life."

"I thought I could lead any sort of life rather than die," said Walter.

"Yes, our flesh will shrink and tremble at the thought of the Judge we must meet," said Edmund; "but He is a gracious Judge, and He knows that it is rather than turn from our duty that we are exposed to death. We may have a good hope, sinners as we are in His sight, that He will grant us His mercy, and be with us when the time comes. But it is late, Walter, we ought to rest, to fit ourselves for what may come to-morrow."

Edmund knelt in prayer, his young brother feeling meantime both sorrowful and humiliated, loving Edmund and admiring him heartily, following what he had said, grieving and rebelling at the fate prepared for him, and at the same time sensible of shame at having so far fallen short of all he had hoped to feel and to prove himself in the time of trial. He had been of very little use to Edmund; his rash interference had only done harm, and added to his mother's distress; he had been nothing but a boy throughout, and instead of being a brave champion, he had been in such an agony of terror at an empty threat, that if the rebel captain had been in the room, he might almost, at one moment, have betrayed his brother. Poor Walter! how he felt what it was never to have learnt self-control!

The brothers arranged themselves for the night without undressing, both occupying Walter's bed. They were both too anxious and excited to sleep, and Walter sat up after a time, listening more calmly to Edmund, who was giving him last messages for Prince Rupert and his other friends, should Walter ever meet them, and putting much in his charge, as now likely to become heir of Woodley Hall and Forest Lea, warning him earnestly to protect his mother and sisters, and be loyal to his King, avoiding all compromise with the enemies of the Church.

Charlotte M. Yonge

CHAPTER VII.

Forest Lea that night was a house of sorrow: the mother and two sons were prisoners in their separate rooms, and the anxieties for the future were dreadful. Rose longed to see and help her mother, dreading the effect of such misery, to be borne in loneliness, by the weak frame, shattered by so many previous sufferings. How was she to undergo all that might yet be in store for her - imprisonment, ill-treatment, above all, the loss of her eldest son? For there was little hope for Edmund. As a friend and follower of Prince Rupert, he was a marked man; and besides, Algernon Sydney, the commander of the nearest body of forces, was known to be a good deal under the influence of the present owner of Woodley, who was likely to be glad to see the rightful heir removed from his path.

Rose perceived all this, and her heart failed her, but she had no time to pause on the thought. The children must be soothed and put to bed, and a hard matter it was to comfort poor little Lucy, perhaps the most of all to be pitied. She relieved herself by pouring out the whole confession to Rose, crying bitterly, while Eleanor hurried on distressing questions whether they would take mamma away, and what they would do to Edmund. Now it came back to Lucy, "O if I had but minded what mamma said about keeping my tongue in order; but now it is too late!"

Rose, after doing her best to comfort them, and listening as near to her mother's door as she dared, to hear if she were weeping, went to her own room. It adjoined Walter's, though the doors did not open into the same passage; and she shut that which closed in the long gallery, where her room and that of her sisters were, so that the Roundhead sentry might not be able to look down it.

As soon as she was in her own room, she threw herself on her knees, and prayed fervently for help and support in their dire distress. In the stillness, as she knelt, she heard an interchange of voices, which she knew must be those of her brothers in the next room. She went nearer to that side, and heard them more distinctly. She was even able to distinguish when Edmund spoke, and when Walter broke forth in impatient exclamations. A sudden thought struck her. She might be able to join in the conversation. There had once been a door between the two rooms, but it had long since been stopped up, and the recess of the doorway was occupied by a great oaken cupboard, in which were preserved all the old stores of rich farthingales of brocade, and velvet mantles, which had been heirlooms from one Dame of Mowbray to another, till poverty had caused them to be cut up and adapted into garments for the little Woodleys.

Rose looked anxiously at the carved doors of the old wardrobe. Had she the key? She felt in her pouch. Yes, she had not given it back to her mother since taking out the sheets for Mr. Enderby. She unlocked the folding doors, and, pushing aside some of the piles of old garments, saw a narrow line of light between the boards, and heard the tones almost as clearly as if she was in the same room.

Charlotte M. Yonge

Eager to tell Edmund how near she was, she stretched herself out, almost crept between the shelves, leant her head against the board on the opposite side, and was about to speak, when she found that it yielded in some degree to her touch. A gleam of hope darted across her, she drew back, fetched her light, tried with her hand, and found that the back of the cupboard was in fact a door, secured on her side by a wooden bolt, which there was no difficulty in undoing. Another push, and the door yielded below, but only so as to show that there must be another fastening above. Rose clambered up the shelves, and sought. Here it was! It was one of the secret communications that were by no means uncommon in old halls in those times of insecurity. Edmund might yet be saved! Trembling with the excess of her delight in her new-found hope, she forced out the second bolt, and pushed again. The door gave way, the light widened upon her, and she saw into the room! Edmund was lying on the bed, Walter sitting at his feet.

Both started as what had seemed to be part of the wainscoted wall opened, but Edmund prevented Walter's exclamation by a sign to be silent, and the next moment Rose's face was seen squeezing between the shelves.

"Edmund! Can you get through here?" she exclaimed in a low eager whisper.

Edmund was immediately by her side, kissing the flushed anxious forehead: "My gallant Rose!" he said.

"Oh, thank heaven! thank heaven! now you may be safe!" continued Rose, still in the same whisper. "I never knew this was a door till this moment. Heaven sent the discovery on purpose for your safety! Hush, Walter! Oh remember the soldier outside!" as Walter was about to break out into tumultuous tokens of gladness. "But can you get through, Edmund? Or perhaps we might move out some of the shelves."

"That is easily done," said Edmund; "but I know not. Even if I should escape, it would be only to fall into the hands of some fresh troop of enemies, and I cannot go and leave my mother to their mercy."

"You could do nothing to save her," said Rose, "and all that they may do to her would scarcely hurt her if she thought you were safe. O Edmund! think of her joy in finding you were escaped! the misery of her anxiety now!"

"Yet to leave her thus! You had not told me half the change in her! I know not how to go!" said Edmund.

"You must, you must!" said Rose and Walter, both at once. And Rose added, "Your death would kill her, I do believe!"

"Well, then; but I do not see my way even when I have squeezed between your shelves, my little sister. Every port is beset, and our hiding places here can no longer serve me."

"Listen," said Rose, "this is what my mother and I had planned before. The old clergyman of this parish, Dr. Bathurst, lives in a little house at Bosham, with his daughter, and maintains himself by teaching the wealthier boys of the town. Now, if you could ride to him to-night, he would be most glad to serve you, both as a cavalier, and for my mother's sake. He would find some place of concealment, and watch for the time when you may attempt to cross the Channel."

Edmund considered, and made her repeat her explanation. "Yes, that might answer," he said at length; "I take you for my general, sweet Rose. But how am I to find your good doctor?"

"I think," said Rose, after considering a little while, "that I had better go with you. I could ride behind you on your horse, if the rebels have not found him, and I know the town, and Dr. Bathurst's lodging. I only cannot think what is to be done about Walter."

"Never mind me," said Walter, "they cannot hurt me."

"Not if you will be prudent, and not provoke them," said Edmund.

"Oh, I know!" cried Rose; "wear my gown and hood! these men have only seen us by candle-light, and will never find you out if you will only be careful."

"I wear girl's trumpery!" exclaimed Walter, in such indignation that Edmund smiled, saying, "If Rose's wit went with her gown, you might be glad of it."

"She is a good girl enough," said Walter, "but as to my putting on her petticoat trash, that's all nonsense."

"Hear me this once, dear Walter," pleaded Rose. "If there is a pursuit, and they fancy you and Edmund are gone together, it will quite mislead them to hear only of a groom riding before a young lady."

"There is something in that," said Walter, "but a pretty

sort of lady I shall make!"

"Then you consent? Thank you, dear Walter. Now, will you help me into your room, and I'll put two rolls of clothes to bed, that the captain may find his prisoners fast asleep to-morrow morning."

Walter could hardly help laughing aloud with delight at the notion of the disappointment of the rebels. The next thing was to consider of Edmund's equipment; Rose turned over her ancient hoards in vain, everything that was not too remarkable had been used for the needs of the family, and he must go in his present blood-stained buff coat, hoping to enter Bosham too early in the morning for gossips to be astir. Then she dressed Walter in her own clothes, not without his making many faces of disgust, especially when she fastened his long curled love-locks in a knot behind, tried to train little curls over the sides of his face, and drew her black silk hood forward so as to shade it. They were nearly of the same height and complexion, and Edmund pronounced that Walter made a very pretty girl, so like Rose that he should hardly have known them apart, which seemed to vex the boy more than all.

There had been a sort of merriment while this was doing, but when it was over, and the moment came when the brother and sister must set off, there was lingering, sorrow, and reluctance. Edmund felt severely the leaving his mother in the midst of peril, brought upon her for his sake, and his one brief sight of his home had made him cling the closer to it, and stirred up in double force the affections for mother, brothers, and sisters, which, though never extinct, had been comparatively dormant while he was engaged in

Charlotte M. Yonge

stirring scenes abroad. Now that he had once more seen the gentle loving countenance of his mother, and felt her tender, tearful caress, known that noble-minded Rose, and had a glimpse of those pretty little sisters, there was such a yearning for them through his whole being, that it seemed to him as if he might as well die as continue to be cast up and down the world far from them.

Rose felt as if she was abandoning her mother by going from home at such a time, when perhaps she should find on her return that she had been carried away to prison. She could not bear to think of being missed on such a morning that was likely to ensue, but she well knew that the greatest good she could do would be to effect the rescue of her brother, and she could not hesitate a moment. She crowded charge after charge upon Walter, with many a message for her mother, promise to return as soon as possible, and entreaty for pardon for leaving her in such a strait; and Edmund added numerous like parting greetings, with counsel and entreaties that she would ask for Colonel Enderby's interference, which might probably avail to save her from further imprisonment and sequestration.

"Good-bye, Walter. In three or four years, if matters are not righted before that, perhaps, if you can come to me, I may find employment for you in Prince Rupert's fleet, or the Duke of York's troop."

"O Edmund, thanks! that would be -"

Walter had not time to finish, for Rose kissed him, left her love and duty to her mother with him, bade him remember he was a lady, and then holding Edmund by

the hand, both with their shoes off, stole softly down
the stairs in the dark.

Charlotte M. Yonge

CHAPTER VIII.

After pacing up and down Rose's room till he was tired, Walter sat down to rest, for Rose had especially forbidden him to lie down, lest he should derange his hair. He grew very sleepy, and at last, with his arms crossed on the table, and his forehead resting on them, fell sound asleep, and did not awaken till it was broad daylight, and calls of "Rose! Rose!" were heard outside the locked door.

He was just going to call out that Rose was not here, when he luckily recollected that he was Rose, pulled his hood forward, and opened the door.

He was instantly surrounded by the three children, who, poor little things, feeling extremely forlorn and desolate without their mother, all gathered round him, Lucy and Eleanor seizing each a hand, and Charles clinging to the skirts of his dress. He by no means understood this; and Rose was so used to it, as to have forgotten he would not like it. "How you crowd?" he exclaimed.

"Mistress Rose," began Deborah, coming half way up stairs - Lucy let go his hand, but Charles instantly grasped it, and he felt as if he could not move. "Don't be troublesome, children," said he, trying to shake them off; "can't you come near one without pulling off one's hands?"

"Mistress!" continued Deborah; but as he forgot he was addressed, and did not immediately attend, she exclaimed, "Oh, she won't even look at me! I thought she had forgiven me."

"Forgiven you!" said he, starting. "Stuff and nonsense; what's all this about? You were a fool, that's all."

Deborah stared at this most unwonted address on the part of her young lady; and Lucy, a sudden light breaking on her, smiled at Eleanor, and held up her finger. Deborah proceeded with her inquiry: "Mistress Rose, shall I take some breakfast to my lady, and the young gentlemen, poor souls?"

"Yes, of course," he answered. "No, wait a bit. Only to my mother, I mean, just at present."

"And the soldiers," continued Deborah - "they're roaring for breakfast; what shall I give them?"

"A halter," he had almost said, but he caught himself up in time, and answered, "What you can - bread, beef, beer -"

"Bread! beef! beer!" almost shrieked Deborah, "when she knows the colonel man had the last of our beer; beef we have not seen for two Christmases, and bread, there's barely enough for my lady and the children, till we bake."

"Well, whatever there is, then," said Walter, anxious to get rid of her.

Charlotte M. Yonge

"I could fry some bacon," pursued Deborah, "only I don't know whether to cut the new flitch so soon; and there be some cabbages in the garden. Should I fry or boil them, Mistress Rose? The bottom is out of the frying-pan, and the tinker is not come this way."

The tinker was too much for poor Walter's patience, and flinging away from her, he exclaimed, "Mercy on me, woman, you'll plague the life out of me!"

Poor Deborah stood aghast. "Mistress Rose! what is it? you look wildly, I declare, and your hood is all I don't know how. Shall I set it right?"

"Mind your own business, and I'll mind mine!" cried Walter.

"Alack! alack!" lamented Deborah, as she hastily retreated down stairs, Charlie running after her. "Mistress Rose is gone clean demented with trouble, and that is the worst that has befallen this poor house yet."

"There!" said Lucy, as soon as she was gone; "I have held my tongue this time. O Walter, you don't do it a bit like Rose!"

"Where is Rose!" said Eleanor. "How did you get out?"

"Well!" said Walter, "it is hard that, whatever we do, women and babies are mixed up with it. I must trust you since you have found me out, but mind, Lucy, not one word or look that can lead anyone to guess what I am telling you. Edmund is safe out of this house, Rose is gone with him - 'tis safest not to say where."

"But is not she coming back?" asked Eleanor.

"Oh yes, very soon - to-day, or to-morrow perhaps. So I am Rose till she comes back, and little did I guess what I was undertaking! I never was properly thankful till now that I was not born a woman!"

"Oh don't stride along so, or they will find you out," exclaimed Eleanor.

"And don't mince and amble, that is worse!" added Lucy. "Oh you will make me laugh in spite of everything."

"Pshaw! I shall shut myself into my - her room, and see nobody!" said Walter; "you must keep Charlie off, Lucy, and don't let Deb drive me distracted. I dare say, if necessary, I can fool it enough for the rebels, who never spoke to a gentlewoman in their lives."

"But only tell me, how did you get out?" said Lucy.

"Little Miss Curiosity must rest without knowing," said Walter, shutting the door in her face.

"Now, don't be curious, dear Lucy," said Eleanor, taking her hand. "We shall know in time."

"I will not, I am not," said Lucy, magnanimously. "We will not say one single word, Eleanor, and I will not look as if I knew anything. Come down, and we will see if we can do any of Rose's work, for we must be very useful, you know; I wish I might tell poor Deb that Edmund is safe."

Walter was wise in secluding himself in his disguise.

He remained undisturbed for some time, while Deborah's unassisted genius was exerted to provide the rebels with breakfast. The first interruption was from Eleanor, who knocked at the door, beginning to call "Walter," and then hastily turning it into "Rose!" He opened, and she said, with tears in her eyes, "O Walter, Walter, the wicked men are really going to take dear mother away to prison. She is come down with her cloak and hood on, and is asking for you - Rose I mean - to wish good-bye. Will you come?"

"Yes," said Walter; "and Edmund -"

"They were just sending up to call him," said Eleanor; "they will find it out in -"

Eleanor's speech was cut short by a tremendous uproar in the next room. "Ha! How? Where are they? How now? Escaped!" with many confused exclamations, and much trampling of heavy boots. Eleanor stood frightened, Walter clapped his hands, cut a very unfeminine caper, clenched his fist, and shook it at the wall, and exclaimed in an exulting whisper, "Ha! ha! my fine fellows! You may look long enough for him!" then ran downstairs at full speed, and entered the hall. His mother, dressed for a journey, stood by the table; a glance of hope and joy lighting on her pale features, but her swollen eyelids telling of a night of tears and sleeplessness. Lucy and Charles were by her side, the front door open, and the horses were being led up and down before it. Walter and Eleanor hurried up to her, but before they had time to speak, the rebel captain dashed into the room, exclaiming, "Thou treacherous woman, thou shalt abye this! Here! mount, pursue, the nearest road to the coast. Smite them rather than let them escape. The malignant nursling of the bloodthirsty Palatine at large again! Follow, and overtake, I say!"

"Which way, sir?" demanded the corporal.

"The nearest to the coast. Two ride to Chichester, two to Gosport. Or here! Where is that maiden, young in years, but old in wiles? Ah, there! come hither, maiden. Wilt thou purchase grace for thy mother by telling which way the prisoners are fled? I know thy wiles, and will visit them on thee and on thy father's house, unless thou dost somewhat to merit forgiveness."

"What do you mean?" demanded Walter, swelling with passion.

"Do not feign, maiden. Thy heart is rejoicing that the enemies of the righteous are escaped."

"You are not wrong there, sir," said Walter.

"I tell thee," said the captain, sternly, "thy joy shall be turned to mourning. Thou shalt see thy mother thrown into a dungeon, and thou and thy sisters shall beg your bread, unless -"

Walter could not endure these empty threats, and exclaimed, "You know you have no power to do this. Is this what you call manliness to use such threats to a poor girl in your power? Out upon you!"

"Ha!" said the rebel, considerably surprised at the young lady's manner of replying. "Is it thus the malignants breed up their daughters, in insolence as well as deceit?"

Charlotte M. Yonge

The last word made Walter entirely forget his assumed character, and striking at the captain with all his force, he exclaimed, "Take that, for giving the lie to a gentleman."

"How now?" cried the rebel, seizing his arm. Walter struggled, the hood fell back. "'Tis the boy! Ha! deceived again! Here! search the house instantly, every corner. I will not be balked a second time."

He rushed out of the room, while Walter, rending off the hood, threw himself into his mother's arms, exclaiming, "O mother dear, I bore it as long as I could."

"My dear rash boy!" said she. "But is he safe? No, do not say where. Thanks, thanks to heaven. Now I am ready for anything!" and so indeed her face proved.

"All owing to Rose, mother; she will soon be back again, she - but I'll say no more, for fear. He left love - duty - Rose left all sorts of greetings, that I will tell you by and by. Ha! do you hear them lumbering about the house? They fancy he is hid there! Yes, you are welcome -"

"Hush! hush, Walter! the longer they look the more time he will gain," whispered his mother. "Oh this is joy indeed!"

"Mamma, I found out Walter, and said not one word," interposed Lucy; but there was no more opportunity for converse permitted, for the captain returned, and ordered the whole party into the custody of a soldier, who was not to lose sight of any of them till the search was completed.

After putting the whole house in disorder, and seeking in vain through the grounds, the captain himself, and one of his men, went off to scour the neighbouring country, and examine every village on the coast.

Lady Woodley and her three younger children were in the meantime locked into her room, while the soldier left in charge was ordered not to let Walter for a moment out of his sight; and both she and Walter were warned that they were to be carried the next morning to Chichester, to answer for having aided and abetted the escape of the notorious traitor, Edmund Woodley.

It was plain that he really meant it, but hope for Edmund made Lady Woodley cheerful about all she might have to undergo; and even trust that the poor little ones she was obliged to leave behind, might be safe with Rose and Deborah. Her great fear was lest the rebels should search the villages before Edmund had time to escape.

Charlotte M. Yonge

CHAPTER IX.

Cautiously stealing down stairs, Rose first, to spy where the rebels might be, the brother and sister reached the kitchen, where Rose provided Edmund with a grey cloak, once belonging to a former serving-man, and after a short search in an old press, brought out various equipments, saddle, belt, and skirt, with which her mother had once been wont to ride pillion-fashion. These they carried to the outhouse where Edmund's horse had been hidden; and when all was set in order by the light of the lantern, Rose thought that her brother looked more like a groom and less like a cavalier than she had once dared to hope. They mounted, and on they rode, across the downs, through narrow lanes, past farm houses, dreading that each yelping dog might rouse his master to report which way they were gone. It was not till day had dawned, and the eastern sky was red with the approaching sun, that they came down the narrow lane that led to the little town of Bosham, a low flat place, sloping very gradually to the water. Here Rose left her brother, advising him to keep close under the hedge, while she softly opened a little gate, and entered a garden, long and narrow, with carefully cultivated flowers and vegetables. At the end was a low cottage; and going up to the door, Rose knocked gently. The door was presently cautiously opened by a girl a few years older, very plainly dressed, as if busy in household work. She started with surprise, then held out her hand, which Rose pressed affectionately, as she said, "Dear Anne, will you tell your father that I should be very glad to speak to him?"

"I will call him," said Anne; "he is just rising. What is - But I will not delay."

"Oh no, do not, thank you, I cannot tell you now." Rose was left by Anne Bathurst standing in a small cleanly-sanded kitchen, with a few wooden chairs neatly ranged, some trenchers and pewter dishes against the wall, and nothing like decoration except a beau-pot, as Anne would have called it, filled with flowers. Here the good doctor and his daughter lived, and tried to eke out a scanty maintenance by teaching a little school.

After what was really a very short interval, but which seemed to Rose a very long one, Dr. Bathurst, a thin, spare, middle-aged man, with a small black velvet cap over his grey hair, came down the creaking rough wooden stairs. "My dear child," he asked, "in what can I help you? Your mother is well, I trust."

"Oh yes, sir!" said Rose; and with reliance and hope, as if she had been speaking to a father, she explained their distress and perplexity, then stood in silence while the good doctor, a slow thinker, considered.

"First, to hide him," he said; "he may not be here, for this - the old parson's house - will be the very first spot they will search. But we will try. You rode, you say, Mistress Rose; where is your horse?"

"Ah! there is one difficulty," said Rose, "Edmund is

holding him now; but where shall we leave him?"

"Let us come first to see the young gentleman," said Dr. Bathurst; and they walked together to the lane where Edmund was waiting, the doctor explaining by the way that he placed his chief dependence on Harry Fletcher, a fisherman, thoroughly brave, trustworthy, and loyal, who had at one time been a sailor, and had seen, and been spoken to by King Charles himself. He lived in a little lonely hut about half a mile distant; he was unmarried, and would have been quite alone, but that he had taken a young nephew, whose father had been killed on the Royalist side, to live with him, and to be brought up to his fishing business.

Edmund and Rose both agreed that there could be no better hope of escape than in trusting to this good man; and as no time was to be lost, they parted for the present, Rose returning to the cottage to spend the day with Anne Bathurst, and the clergyman walking with the young cavalier to the place where the fisherman lived. They led the horse with them for some distance, then tied him to a gate, a little out of sight, and went on to the hut, which stood, built of the shingle of the beach, just beyond the highest reach of the tide, with the boat beside it, and the nets spread out to dry.

Before there was time to knock, the door was opened by Harry Fletcher himself, his open sunburnt face showing honesty and good faith in every feature. He put his hand respectfully to his woollen cap, and said, with a sort of smile, as he looked at Edmund, "I see what work you have for me, your reverence."

"You are right, Harry," said Dr. Bathurst; "this is one of the gentlemen that fought for his Majesty at

Worcester, and if we cannot get him safe out of the country, with heaven's blessing, he is as good as a dead man."

"Come in, sir," said Fletcher, "you had best not be seen. There's no one here but little Dick, and I'll answer for him."

They came in, and Dr. Bathurst explained Edmund's circumstances. The honest fellow looked a little perplexed, but after a moment said, "Well, I'll do what in me lies, sir; but 'tis a long way across."

"I should tell you, my good man," said Edmund, "that I have nothing to repay you with for all the trouble and danger to which you may be exposing yourself on my behalf. Nothing but my horse, which would only be bringing suspicion on you."

"As to that, your honour," replied Harry, "I'd never think of waiting for pay in a matter of life and death. I am glad if I can help off a gentleman that has been on the King's side."

So the plan was arranged. Edmund was to be disguised in the fisherman's clothes, spend the day at his hut, and at night, if the weather served, Fletcher would row him out to sea, assisted by the little boy, in hopes of falling in with a French vessel; or, if not, they must pull across to Havre or Dieppe. The doctor promised to bring Rose at ten o'clock to meet him on the beach and bid him farewell. As to the horse, Fletcher sent the little boy to turn it out on the neighbouring down, and hide the saddle.

All this arranged, Dr. Bathurst returned to his school;

and Rose, dressed in Anne's plainest clothes, rested on her bed as long as her anxiety would allow her, then came down and helped in her household work. It was well that Rose was thus employed, for in the afternoon they had a great fright. Two soldiers came knocking violently at the door, exhibiting an order to search for the escaped prisoner. Rose recognised two of the party who had been at Forest Lea; but happily they had not seen enough of her to know her in the coarse blue stuff petticoat that she now wore. One of them asked who she was, and Anne readily replied, "Oh, a friend who is helping me;" after which they paid her no further attention.

Her anxiety for Edmund was of course at its height during this search, and it was not till the evening that she could gain any intelligence. Edmund's danger had indeed been great. Harry Fletcher saw the rebels coming in time to prepare. He advised his guest not to remain in the house, as if he wished to avoid observation, but to come out, as if afraid of nothing. His cavalier dress had been carefully destroyed or concealed; he wore the fisherman's rough clothes, and had even sacrificed his long dark hair, covering his head with one of Harry's red woollen caps. He was altogether so different in appearance from what he had been yesterday, that he ventured forward, and leant whistling against the side of the boat, while Harry parleyed with the soldiers. Perhaps they suspected Harry a little, for they insisted on searching his hut, and as they were coming out, one of them began to tell him of the penalties that fishermen would incur by favouring the escape of the Royalists. Harry did not lose countenance, but went on hammering at his boat as if he cared not at all, till observing that one of the soldiers was looking hard at Edmund, he called out, "I say, Ned, what's the use of loitering there, listening to what's no concern of yours? Fetch the oar out of yon shed. I never lit on such a lazy comrade in my life."

This seemed to turn away all suspicion, the soldiers left them, and no further mischance occurred. At night, just as the young moon was setting, the boat was brought out, and Harry, with little Dick and a comrade whom he engaged could be trusted, prepared their oars. At the same time, Dr. Bathurst and Rose came silently to meet them along the shingly beach. Rose hardly knew her brother in his fisherman's garb. The time was short, and their hearts were too full for many words, as that little party stood together in the light of the crescent moon, the sea sounding with a low constant ripple, spread out in the grey hazy blue distance, and here and there the crests of the nearer waves swelling up and catching the moonlight.

Edmund and his sister held their hands tightly clasped, loving each other, if possible, better than ever. He now and then repeated some loving greeting which she was to bear home; and she tried to restrain her tears, at the separation she was forced to rejoice in, a parting which gave no augury of meeting again, the renewal of an exile from which there was no present hope of return. Harry looked at Dr. Bathurst to intimate it was time to be gone. The clergyman came close to the brother and sister, and instead of speaking his own words, used these:-

"Turn our captivity, O LORD, as the rivers in the south."

"They that sow in tears shall reap in joy."

"He that now goeth on his way weeping, and beareth forth good seed, shall doubtless come again with joy, and bring his sheaves with him."

"Amen," answered Edmund and Rose; and they loosened their hold of each other with hearts less sore. Then Edmund bared his head, and knelt down, and the good clergyman called down a blessing from heaven on him; Harry, the faithful man who was going to risk himself for him, did the same, and received the same blessing. There were no more words, the boat pushed off, and the splash of the oars resounded regularly.

Rose's tears came thick, fast, blinding, and she sat down on a block of wood and wept long and bitterly; then she rose up, and in answer to Dr. Bathurst's cheering words, she said, "Yes, I do thank GOD with all my heart!"

That night Rose slept at Dr. Bathurst's, and early in the morning was rejoiced by the tidings which Harry Fletcher sent little Dick to carry to the cottage. The voyage had been prosperous, they had fallen in with a French vessel, and Mr. Edmund Woodley had been safely received on board.

She was very anxious to return home; and as it was Saturday, and therefore a holiday at the school, Dr. Bathurst undertook to go with her and spend the Sunday at Forest Lea. One of the farmers of Bosham helped them some little way with his harvest cart, but the rest of the journey had to be performed on foot. It was not till noon that they came out upon the high road between Chichester and Forest Lea; and they had not been upon it more than ten minutes, before the sound of horses' tread was heard, as if coming from

Chichester. Looking round, they saw a gentleman riding fast, followed by a soldier also on horseback. There was something in his air that Rose recognised, and as he came nearer she perceived it was Sylvester Enderby. He was much amazed, when, at the same moment, he perceived it was Mistress Rose Woodley, and stopping his horse, and taking off his hat, with great respect both towards her and the clergyman, he hoped all the family were well in health.

"Yes, yes, I believe so, thank you," replied Rose, looking anxiously at him.

"I am on my way to Forest Lea," he said. "I bring the order my father hoped to obtain from General Cromwell."

"The Protection! Oh, thanks! ten thousand thanks!" cried Rose. "Oh! it may save - But hasten on, pray hasten on, sir. The soldiers are already at home; I feared she might be already a prisoner at Chichester. Pray go on and restrain them by your authority. Don't ask me to explain - you will understand all when you are there."

She prevailed on him to go on, while she, with Dr. Bathurst, more slowly proceeded up the chalky road which led to the summit of the green hill or down, covered with short grass, which commanded a view of all the country round, and whence they would turn off upon the down leading to Forest Lea. Just as they came to the top, Rose cast an anxious glance in the direction of her home, and gave a little cry. Sylvester Enderby and his attendant could be seen speeding down the green slope of the hill; but at some distance further on, was a little troop of horsemen, coming from the direction of Forest Lea, the sun now and then flashing on a steel cap or on the point of a pike. Fast rode on Sylvester, nearer and nearer came the troop; Rose almost fancied she could discern on one of the horses something muffled in black that could be no other than her mother. How she longed for wings to fly to meet her and cheer her heart with the assurance of Edmund's safety! How she longed to be on Sylvester's horse, as she saw the distance between him and the party fast diminishing! At length he was close to it, he had mingled with it; and at the same time Dr. Bathurst and Rose had to mount a slightly rising ground, which for a time entirely obscured their view. When at length they had reached the summit of this eminence, the party were standing still, as if in parley; there was presently a movement, a parting, Rose clasped her hands in earnestness. The main body continued their course to Chichester, a few remained stationary. How many? One, two, three - yes, four, or was it five? and among them the black figure she had watched so anxiously! "She is safe, she is safe!" cried Rose. "Oh, GOD has been so very good to us, I wish I could thank Him enough!"

Leaving the smoother slope to avoid encountering the baffled rebels, Dr. Bathurst and Rose descended the steep, the good man exerting himself that her eagerness might not be disappointed. Down they went, sliding on the slippery green banks, helping themselves with the doctor's trusty staff, taking a short run at the lowest and steepest part of each, creeping down the rude steps, or rather foot-holes, cut out by the shepherd-boys in the more perpendicular descents, and fairly sliding or running down the shorter ones. They saw their friends waiting for them; and a lesser figure than the rest hastened towards them, scaling the steep slopes with a good will, precipitancy, and wild hurrahs of exultation, that would not let them doubt it was Walter, before they could see his form distinctly, or hear his words. Rose ran headlong down the last green slope, and was saved from falling by fairly rushing into his arms.

"Is he safe? I need not ask!" exclaimed Walter.

"Safe! in a French vessel. And mother?"

"Safe! well! happy! You saw, you heard! Hurrah! The crop-ears are sent to the right about; the captain has done mother and me the favour to forgive us, as a Christian, all that has passed, he says. We are all going home again as fast as we can, young Enderby and all, to chase out the two rogues that are quartered on us to afflict poor Deb and the little ones."

By this time Dr. Bathurst had descended, more cautiously, and Walter went to greet him, and repeat his news. Together they proceeded to meet the rest; and who can tell the tearful happiness when Rose and her mother were once more pressed in each other's arms!

"My noble girl! under Providence you have saved him!" whispered Lady Woodley.

The next evening, in secrecy, with the shutters shut, and the light screened, the true pastor of Forest Lea gathered the faithful ones of his flock for a service in the old hall. There knelt many a humble, loyal, trustful peasant; there was the widowed Dame Ewins, trying to be comforted, as they told her she ought; there was the lady herself, at once sorrowful and yet earnestly thankful; there was Sylvester Enderby, hearing and following the prayers he had been used to in his early childhood, with a growing feeling that here lay the right and the truth; there was Deborah, weeping, grieving over her own fault, and almost heart-broken at the failure of him on whom she had set her warm affections, yet perhaps in a way made wiser, and taught to trust no longer to a broken reed, but to look for better things; there were Walter and Lucy, both humbled and subdued, repenting in earnest of the misbehaviour each of them had been guilty of. Walter did not show his contrition much in manner, but it was real, and he proved it by many a struggle with his self-willed overbearing temper. It was a real resolution that he took now, and in a spirit of humility, which made him glad to pray that what was past might be forgiven, and that he might be helped for the future. That was the first time Walter had ever kept up his attention through the whole service, but it all came home to him now.

Each of that little congregation had their own sorrow of heart, their own prayer and thanksgiving, to pour out in secret; but all could join in one thank-offering for the safety of the heir of that house; all joined in one prayer for the rescue of their hunted King, and for the restoration of their oppressed and afflicted Church.

* * *

Nine years had passed away, and Forest Lea still stood among the stumps of its cut-down trees; but one fair long day in early June there was much that was changed in its aspect. The park was carefully mown and swept; the shrubs were trained back; the broken windows were repaired; and within the hall the appearance of everything was still more strikingly cheerful, as the setting sun looked smilingly in at the western window. Green boughs filled the hearth, and were suspended round the walls; fresh branches of young oak leaves, tasselled with the pale green catkins; the helmets and gauntlets hanging on the wall were each adorned with a spray, and polished to the brightest; the chairs and benches were ranged round the long table, covered with a spotless cloth, and bearing in the middle a large bowl filled with oak boughs, roses, lilac, honey-suckle, and all the pride of the garden.

At the head of the table sat, less pale, and her face beaming with deep, quiet, heartfelt joy, Lady Woodley herself; and near her were Dr. Bathurst and his happy daughter, who in a few days more were to resume their abode in his own parsonage. Opposite to her was a dark soldierly sun-burnt man, on whose countenance toil, weather, and privation had set their traces, but whose every tone and smile told of the ecstasy of being once more at home.

Merry faces were at each side of the table; Walter, grown up into a tall noble-looking youth of two-and-twenty, particularly courteous and gracious in demeanour, and most affectionate to his mother; Charles, a gentle sedate boy of fifteen, so much given to books and gravity, that his sisters called him their little scholar; Rose, with the same sweet thoughtful face, active step, and helpful hand, that she had always possessed, but very pale, and more pensive and grave than became a time of rejoicing, as if the cares and toils of her youth had taken away her light heart, and had given her a soft subdued melancholy that was always the same. She was cheerful when others were cast down and overwhelmed; but when they were gay, she, though not sorrowful, seemed almost grave, in spite of her sweet smiles and ready sympathy. Yet Rose was very happy, no less happy than Eleanor, with her fair, lovely, laughing face, or -

"But where is Lucy?" Edmund asked, as he saw her chair vacant.

"Lucy?" said Rose; "she will come in a moment. She is going to bring in the dish you especially ordered, and which Deborah wonders at."

"Good, faithful Deborah!" said Edmund. "Did she never find a second love?"

"Oh no, never," said Eleanor. "She says she has seen enough of men in her time."

"She is grown sharper than ever," said Walter, "now she is Mistress Housekeeper Deborah; I shall pity the poor maidens under her."

"She will always be kind in the main," rejoined Rose.

"And did you ever hear what became of that precious sweetheart of hers?" asked Edmund.

"Hanged for sheep stealing," replied Walter, "according to the report of Sylvester Enderby. But hush, for enter -"

There entered Lucy, smiling and blushing, her dark hair decorated with the spray of oak, and her hands supporting a great pewter dish, in which stood a noble pie, of pale-brown, well-baked crust, garnished with many a pair of little claws, showing what were the contents. She set it down in the middle of the table, just opposite to Walter. The grace was said, the supper began, and great was the merriment when Walter, raising a whole pigeon on his fork, begged to know if Rose had appetite enough for it, and if she still possessed the spirit of a wolf. "And," said he, as they finished, "now Rose will never gainsay me more when I sing -

"For forty years our Royal throne
Has been his father's and his own,
Nor is there anyone but he
With right can there a sharer be.
For who better may
The right sceptre sway,
Than he whose right it is to reign?
Then look for no peace,
For the war will never cease
Till the King enjoys his own again.

"Then far upon the distant hill
My hope has cast her anchor still,
Until I saw the peaceful dove
Bring home the branch I dearly love.
And there did I wait
Till the waters abate
That did surround my swimming brain;
For rejoice could never I
Till I heard the joyful cry
That the King enjoys his own again!"

Charlotte M. Yonge

Choose from Thousands of 1stWorldLibrary Classics By

Adolphus WilliamWard
Aesop
Agatha Christie
Alexander Aaronsohn
Alexander Kielland
Alexandre Dumas
Alfred Gatty
Alfred Ollivant
Alice Duer Miller
Alice Turner Curtis
Alice Dunbar
Ambrose Bierce
Amelia E. Barr
Andrew Lang
Andrew McFarland Davis
Anna Sewell
Annie Besant
Annie Hamilton Donnell
Annie Payson Call
Anton Chekhov
Arnold Bennett
Arthur Conan Doyle
Arthur Ransome
Atticus
B. M. Bower
Basil King
Bayard Taylor
Ben Macomber
Booth Tarkington
Bram Stoker
C. Collodi
C. E. Orr
C. M. Ingleby
Carolyn Wells
Catherine Parr Traill
Charles A. Eastman
Charles Dickens
Charles Dudley Warner
Charles Farrar Browne
Charles Ives
Charles Kingsley
Charles Lathrop Pack
Charles Whibley
Charles Willing Beale
Charlotte M. Braeme
Charlotte M.Yonge
Clair W. Hayes
Clarence Day Jr.
Clarence E. Mulford

Clemence Housman
Confucius
Cornelis DeWitt Wilcox
Cyril Burleigh
D. H. Lawrence
Daniel Defoe
David Garnett
Don Carlos Janes
Donald Keyhole
Dorothy Kilner
Dougan Clark
E. Nesbit
E.P.Roe
E. Phillips Oppenheim
Edgar Allan Poe
Edgar Rice Burroughs
Edith Wharton
Edward J. O'Biren
John Cournos
Edwin L. Arnold
Eleanor Atkins
Elizabeth Cleghorn
Gaskell
Elizabeth Von Arnim
Ellem Key
Emily Dickinson
Erasmus W. Jones
Ernie Howard Pie
Ethel Turner
Ethel Watts Mumford
Eugenie Foa
Eugene Wood
Evelyn Everett-Green
Everard Cotes
F. J. Cross
Federick Austin Ogg
Ferdinand Ossendowski
Francis Bacon
Francis Darwin
Frances Hodgson Burnett
Frank Gee Patchin
Frank Harris
Frank Jewett Mather
Frank L. Packard
Frederick Trevor Hill
Frederick Winslow Taylor
Friedrich Kerst
Friedrich Nietzsche
Fyodor Dostoyevsky

Gabrielle E. Jackson
Garrett P. Serviss
Gaston Leroux
George Ade
Geroge Bernard Shaw
George Ebers
George Eliot
George MacDonald
George Orwell
George Tucker
George W. Cable
George Wharton James
Gertrude Atherton
Grace E. King
Grant Allen
Guillermo A. Sherwell
Gulielma Zollinger
Gustav Flaubert
H. A. Cody
H. B. Irving
H. G. Wells
H. H. Munro
H. Irving Hancock
H. Rider Haggard
H. W. C. Davis
Hamilton Wright Mabie
Hans Christian Andersen
Harold Avery
Harold McGrath
Harriet Beecher Stowe
Harry Houidini
Helent Hunt Jackson
Helen Nicolay
Hendy David Thoreau
Henrik Ibsen
Henry Adams
Henry Ford
Henry Frost
Henry James
Henry Jones Ford
Henry Seton Merriman
Henry Wadsworth
Longfellow
Henry W Longfellow
Herbert A. Giles
Herbert N. Casson
Herman Hesse
Homer
Honore De Balzac

Horace Walpole
Horatio Alger, Jr.
Howard Pyle
Howard R. Garis
Hugh Lofting
Hugh Walpole
Humphry Ward
Ian Maclaren
Israel Abrahams
J.G.Austin
J. Henri Fabre
J. M. Barrie
J. Macdonald Oxley
J. S. Knowles
J. Storer Clouston
Jack London
Jacob Abbott
James Allen
James Lane Allen
James Andrews
James Baldwin
James DeMille
James Joyce
James Oliver Curwood
James Oppenheim
James Otis
Jane Austen
Jens Peter Jacobsen
Jerome K. Jerome
John Burroughs
John F. Kennedy
John Gay
John Glasworthy
John Habberton
John Joy Bell
John Milton
John Philip Sousa
Jonathan Swift
Joseph Carey
Joseph Conrad
Joseph Jacobs
Julian Hawthrone
Julies Vernes
Justin Huntly McCarthy
Kakuzo Okakura
Kenneth Grahame
Kate Langley Bosher
L. A. Abbot
L. T. Meade
L. Frank Baum
Laura Lee Hope

Laurence Housman
Leo Tolstoy
Leonid Andreyev
Lewis Carroll
Lilian Bell
Lloyd Osbourne
Louis Tracy
Louisa May Alcott
Lucy Fitch Perkins
Lucy Maud Montgomery
Lydia Miller Middleton
Lyndon Orr
M. H. Adams
Margaret E. Sangster
Margaret Vandercook
Maria Edgeworth
Maria Thompson Daviess
Mariano Azuela
Marion Polk Angellotti
Mark Overton
Mark Twain
Mary Austin
Mary Cole
Mary Rowlandson
Mary Wollstonecraft
Shelley
Max Beerbohm
Myra Kelly
Nathaniel Hawthrone
O. F. Walton
Oscar Wilde
Owen Johnson
P.G.Wodehouse
Paul and Mable Thorn
Paul G. Tomlinson
Paul Severing
Peter B. Kyne
Plato
R. Derby Holmes
R. L. Stevenson
Rabindranath Tagore
Rahul Alvares
Ralph Waldo Emmerson
Rene Descartes
Rex E. Beach
Richard Harding Davis
Richard Jefferies
Robert Barr
Robert Frost
Robert Gordon Anderson
Robert L. Drake

Robert Lansing
Robert Michael Ballantyne
Robert W. Chambers
Rosa Nouchette Carey
Ross Kay
Rudyard Kipling
Samuel B. Allison
Samuel Hopkins Adams
Sarah Bernhardt
Selma Lagerlof
Sherwood Anderson
Sigmund Freud
Standish O'Grady
Stanley Weyman
Stella Benson
Stephen Crane
Stewart Edward White
Stijn Streuvels
Swami Abhedananda
Swami Parmananda
T. S. Ackland
The Princess Der Ling
Thomas A. Janvier
Thomas A Kempis
Thomas Anderton
Thomas Bailey Aldrich
Thomas Bulfinch
Thomas De Quincey
Thomas H. Huxley
Thomas Hardy
Thomas More
Thornton W. Burgess
U. S. Grant
Valentine Williams
Victor Appleton
Virginia Woolf
Walter Scott
Washington Irving
Wilbur Lawton
Wilkie Collins
Willa Cather
Willard F. Baker
William Makepeace
Thackeray
William W. Walter
Winston Churchill
Yei Theodora Ozaki
Young E. Allison
Zane Grey